The Fat Plan

GLEN NEATH

Portobello
BOOKS

LONDON

Published by Portobello Books Ltd 2008

Portobello Books Ltd
Twelve Addison Avenue
London
W11 4QR, UK

A CIP catalogue record is available from
the British Library

9 8 7 6 5 4 3 2 1

ISBN 978 1 84627 147 2

www.portobellobooks.com

For Sonny John Loudon Neath

the little fat

I am a man of limited powers.

I do not own a car, so I'm stuck here, a prisoner to a certain extent if you like, although I'd like it to be known I wasn't brought here against my will, in fact far from it. And if I ever want to get away I only need to wait for Mr Gatt to arrive in his lovely flash car and I can get a lift back with him. He might not want to take me though, even if I were to ask him, because I signed a contract stipulating I'd remain here for the duration of the job, although he has never made it clear how long that's going to be. I tell myself I'd never have agreed to stay here indefinitely, but then as soon as I remember how I used to live I know I'd have signed up for almost anything. I just needed to get away from my old life, which had become unbearable and would not leave me in peace.

I don't want to suggest I'm unhappy with the situation. I'm not forced to lock myself up in the house, not if I don't want to; I can go for a walk in the fields whenever I like; the house is surrounded by fields, and there's no rule against exploration. Every time it looks like I might step out into nature though, I think, it'll all still be there in the morning, and invariably it is. As for going into the town, I don't need to, I'm provided with all the things I need, my staples are delivered once a week; they appear as if by magic on the step outside my back door.

I am also a man with only a certain amount of physical strength. I mean I'm strong, but only in small concentrated bursts, for example if I am challenged, when the strength is perhaps augmented with adrenalin, and so isn't so much the strength alone as the strength added to; whatever the concentration of it, it's short-lived. I struggle to do a single press-up actually because I'm obese and also because my heart isn't in exercising. I can barely stomach a walk between rooms if I'm honest with myself, because I'm often reminded I'm carrying my body around and it's slowly failing me: in fact I can't forgive it for that, and am generally at war with it, I mean at war in the quietest sense of the word; we ignore each other mainly and I harbour evil thoughts against it on occasion. The body doesn't give me an easy ride either. For example, one day it won't get out of bed, or it bangs itself into one of the sharp corners on the table, on purpose I think. It even put its hand on the hot oven ring but couldn't hold itself there for long; it's true that, for a moment, while the hand was on the stove, I was at the mercy of the body, but when the hand was burnt I only had to not think about running it under the tap and the body was once again beholden to me. The lesson learnt is if it tries to hurt me it hurts itself in the process, and so we have tried to find more novel ways of gaining supremacy over one another. The body mainly attempts to embarrass me in public by passing wind and I have discovered dieting. Over the last few months I've taken forty pounds of the body away from itself; I figure every pound lost is a pound less for it to use against me in the future. I've also taken up smoking again, which leaves me feeling weak in the mornings and starved of oxygen.

As an example of the state of affairs though, this perfectly describes the precarious ceasefire we share, my body and myself.

My body exists out here in isolation with no reason to hold itself in check, unobserved as it mostly is by passers-by and by me also when I am lost in a series of complex thoughts, and so generally it has the run of the place; it's only when I need it to, and am adamant about it, that the body will do what my mind bids it.

But where does all that leave me? It means I don't get out of the house very often, which means I am perfect for this job, because mainly I only have to sit on my fat arse, which suits me fine. There's nothing physical about it but I find I am up and down anyway, I admit it, making tea, sitting down and then getting up again because I can't think about the dirty cup on the kitchen side, and so I'm always washing up and putting things away in cupboards as well, I suppose. I am not, I hasten to add, one of those obsessive-compulsives (is that what they call them?), I mean not being able to leave the dirty cup dirty on the kitchen side – it isn't about hygiene, it's just the work I'm doing can be boring and lonely and often I look for ways of distracting myself from doing it. If I have moments when I wonder what I'm doing here I remember the way things used to be. I knew what was involved when I signed up, and still I happily signed up.

I remember when I first saw the advertisement for the position. I was standing at a bus stop, although I didn't really have anywhere to go, and there it was, attached to the nearest lamppost, a small rectangular card. It read: Want to earn your ideal wage every week, but don't want to work from home? I wrote the contact number down on my hand and turned back, without getting on the bus. I sat in the flat for a couple of hours eating a take-away, smoking, wondering what the job might be and dreaming about what sort of new life a job like this might offer me. Then I tried to visualise a figure I thought might be close to my ideal wage: as it turned out it wasn't such a large figure, after all I certainly wasn't earning anything much now, in fact my whole life was at a dead end. The truth is, I was sorry that I existed at all, a feeling fuelled more by apathy than despair and so consequently of little import, I mean I wasn't going to do anything about it. Nevertheless I hated the fact I was overweight for a start. I also hated the fact my hair was receding, and that my eyes were too close together. Also my lips were too thin, my nose was neither prominent nor petite, my cheeks still bore the craters of teenage acne, and because of a childhood accident I couldn't raise my left arm above my head properly. I hated the fact that if I'd ever had any ambitions they remained unachieved as far as I could tell. I hated the fact that as the years passed me by nothing seemed to change. And I also hated the flat I was living in; I was on the eighth floor of a block and still the view was terrible, which I had always considered unlucky, never mind how unlikely it was: I mean, if you live on the eighth floor you expect a nice view.

After contemplating all of this for a while, and realising I had nothing at all to lose and everything to gain, I called the number. This in itself seemed to me to be a great statement of my new positive intent. The phone only rang once before it was picked up, and so the voice, when it came, took me a little by surprise: Hello, how can I be of help? The voice was super-efficient-sounding. Oh… yes… hello, I stuttered. How can I be of help? The voice had to ask me again. I'm calling about the job, I replied, to which the voice enquired: You saw the advert? I did, I said, on a lamppost. Yes, the voice said, I'm reliably informed it's on lampposts all over the city. It's also featured in certain quality publications. Positions vacant. Yes, of course, I said with some certainty, as if I knew, although I didn't because I existed on a diet of free newspapers, take-away leaflets and the occasional cheap paperback I might come across in a charity shop.

When can you come in? What? Of course we need to meet you, the voice replied tersely. Sure, I said, you mean like an interview? That's right, said the voice, like an interview.

What about tomorrow? I said. The voice was taken aback. Tomorrow? Yes, I have nothing else to do, I said, although of course you can always think of something.

Next Monday would be better, and then after a pause, perhaps in response to my hesitation, the voice said: OK?

Finally I was given an address. It was somewhere I had never heard of. This might be the first test, I thought, to find the place. What with all the excitement, I forgot to ask what the job was.

For the remaining part of that week and over the weekend, before my interview on the Monday morning, I was subjected to mild fits of anxiety, which came over me in waves, or rather ripples. What had I signed myself up to, I wondered. Had I in fact signed up to anything at all yet? I tried to recall what I had revealed to the voice at the other end of the telephone, I mean in terms of clues about my identity. For a start, did I give out my name and address? I thought I must have. If I failed to turn up would they send strong-armed men to look for me? I didn't know. Meanwhile I was buffeted from the inside by rivers of adrenalin; my innards were subject to the same kind of assault a cliff receives from the sea, and as a result by the time the day of the interview arrived my body was worn out and I was able to take full possession of it; in fact I woke up with a new sense of confidence, which I was unable to beat back. All the worries which had plagued me had been dissipated.

I went in search of the address, approaching it down a side road off the main high street, which suddenly opened out onto a car park. The car park was probably once a pretty square, surrounded on all four sides as it was by flats, which had been taken over at street level by boutiques and other retail outlets. The building I was looking for was occupied by a self-storage company: I imagined inside, a labyrinthine muddle of corridors and cages.

Fourth floor, the intercom said to me, and I waited for the buzzer to sound and let me in. When it did I was immediately confronted by a number of steps in the entry hall (only four of them). The landing they ascended to was flanked by two further doors (the one on my left to a toilet, the one ahead of me to I don't know where), and a staircase to my right. I climbed the stairs, finding on each successive landing corridors lined with numbered cages. All the time I was following a series of arrows marked on pieces of paper that had been tacked hurriedly onto the walls. Above the arrows was written the word INTERVIEWS in thick black marker pen.

On the fourth floor I entered through a small portal-like entrance, behind which was another set of stairs, these ones being rickety and enclosed, which carried me upwards in a tight spiral before delivering me on to another landing painted an oppressive grey, the colour of steel filing cabinets. The only door on this landing was to my right and through a panel of mottled glass there was a tantalising promise of natural light. I knocked on the door and entered.

The room I found inside was tiny. There was a photocopier directly inside the door, and to my left shelves from ceiling to floor, stacked high with box files. Beside the photocopier a fax machine sat on a low table, a basket of incoming corres-pondence next to it. The walls were dirty yellow and cracked, plaster was coming away in huge flakes and posters relating to matters of health and safety at work had been tacked up in an effort to obscure the areas showing the worst signs of decrepitude. The carpet was old and tacky underfoot. Facing me there was a desk with a window above it and sitting behind it, a woman reading a magazine. Also in the room was an old man seated on a battered leather sofa. Such was the premium on space the sofa was pushed up almost against the desk. From where the woman was sitting she would only have been able to see the old man's head, sitting on the end of her desk like a wrinkled paperweight.

I have an appointment, I said to the woman without further ado. She smiled. Take a seat. We'll be with you in just a moment.

There was only the sofa to sit on, so I perched myself beside the old man, who adjusted his position slightly as if to make room for me. Facing us was another door, which must have led into a second room where the interviews were being conducted.

I tried to formulate a picture in my mind of a successful conclusion to the forthcoming consultation, which I have been reliably informed is the proper thing to do in circumstances like these. In it the interviewer closed a thin brown folder and added it to a pile of folders already in a tray on the table at their right hand, and this always as the person facing them got to their feet: it was these two actions, when they occurred one shortly after the other that seemed to signify the interview had been terminated; sometimes they would shake hands if either felt a further action was needed and made some effort to instigate it. I gripped the proffered hand firmly and thanked the interviewer. As I stood there, however, in the middle of the handshake, with the interview in the very latter stages of its termination, I gradually became aware my blinks were purposefully slowing themselves down. I feared I might miss the right moment to make my exit and so jeopardise what I believed had been a successful meeting. Actually I was terrified most of all I might fall into a light snooze or become distracted by a particularly absorbing thought, like: I wonder if this really is the first moment at the beginning of a new and better life.

This final exchange is the last obstacle between me and a happier future, I thought (I had already assimilated that piece of information), but unfortunately, with my body already in revolt, my mind turned its attention to thoughts that were not useful to me in this particular situation, such as I began to think of the interviewer as a force unto him- or herself, who used their power like a stick, wielding it against me with glee. Hold on. I am already building a defensive stance in my mind, before the interview has even started. I think maybe, to begin with, a less antagonistic outlook. Look first, when you get the chance, into their eyes and decide from the off whether they've got it in for you. Is it possible I will be able to tell, I wondered. After all, isn't it their job to disguise their feelings? Isn't this what they've been trained to do? Slowly does it then, don't run on ahead of yourself, begin by thinking of them in a warm light, perhaps happy at home with their children; pat one of the children on the head as they pass.

Back in the anteroom I was distracted out of my reverie when the woman behind the desk turned over a page of her magazine. I asked her if there was a lavatory I could use.

I returned a few minutes later to see nothing had moved on during my absence. The older man was still sitting, looking straight ahead. I decided he was imagining a successful interview too, so I sat down heavily in the hope I might distract him and force his interview to end badly. When the time comes, I imagined, and it's me against the old man, I could make an audacious attempt to push in in front of him. I saw it as an opportunity, I think, to somehow return my imagined interview

– that had run on so badly in spite of me – to its rightful and successful conclusion. Yes, I was very confident I could pull it off, after all I was younger, I thought, and lighter now, following my piss, and the older man, weighed down by his years and a bladder full of urine, will have no chance against me. So it would prove, I said to myself.

Actually if anyone should have needed to pee, I mused, it was surely the older man with the older bladder, but he had decided to wait. Fair enough, I told myself.

Anyway I had never been as sure of anything in my life as I was of the facts as I saw them now: Yes, I thought, I could certainly put one over the old man.

A moment or two later the door opened into the interview room next door. The woman looked up from her magazine and got to her feet as a middle-aged woman who didn't look good for her age came out of the office followed by the voice of a man, which was saying: Can you show the next person in please? The receptionist gestured to the old man and he stood and made his way, unmolested, into the office. A lost opportunity then, but one I was never seriously going to entertain. Come in, said a woman's voice from within. as the old man closed the door behind him.

The middle-aged woman meanwhile was standing in front of the desk, her face expressing a mixture of perplexed confusion and – dare I say it? – hope. She blinked momentarily, as if she had just been born again into the real world; all the previous rosy hues she had imagined herself surrounded by were diluted and falling away and diluted again by the light coming in through the window. She looked at the young woman, who had moved out from behind her desk. Is that everything? she wondered. The receptionist informed her that it was, at least as far as she was concerned. We'll let you know, she added. We have all your details. The woman made her way out.

From then on, for most of the next twenty minutes, I thought a lot about a cigarette and in the other free moments, when the urge to smoke subsided, I indulged in unhindered views of the young woman, I mean when she wasn't paying any attention to me I was free to consider her at my leisure. She was very young, perhaps seventeen. I could see that she saw me only as 'the fat man' as she had seen the old man before me purely as 'the old man'. It seemed unfair. On occasion she caught sight of me studying her and when this happened I smiled in an attempt to cover my tracks. Could she tell from my face what I was thinking? Surely not. She was very young and the young misinterpret everything. Had she misinterpreted my smile and taken it to mean something it didn't mean? What did it mean? If I didn't know what it meant what chance did she have? And how could I accuse her of misinterpreting anything? Maybe she could tell me something about myself.

She smiled back but her attempts were risible and looked anything but natural. She had lovely straight teeth though.

Putting aside all my personal considerations, I wondered if I could learn anything from her about the job. But she didn't look to me like she might be a fount of knowledge and besides she was clearly determined to share no intimacies of any kind with me.

We sat in silence.

When it was finally my turn the old man had just left and I stepped through the door, which he had left ajar. I heard a few mumbled pleasantries between him and the receptionist behind me and tried to block them out of my mind because I was across the threshold into the room within, which wasn't much larger than the room without, I soon realised. It too was an unremarkable room, not only in respect of this, but in every other respect. There was a window on my left, a blind over it pulled halfway down. On the wall was a print of a landscape, a field obscured by red poppies. A woman with a parasol was walking in the long grass. The sun, a hazy yellow impasto ball in the sky, beat down on her mercilessly. There were only a number of birds, circling overhead, to note her existence at all.

Beside a filing cabinet in the corner a man, who had been on his feet to see the old man exit and me enter in his place, was making himself comfortable again to one side of a woman holding court behind the desk, which was clear of almost everything except a few sheets of paper in two piles and a fountain pen, which she picked up before saying good morning to me. This then is my interviewer, I thought. I sat down opposite her.

Good morning, I said in reply. I nodded at the man and he

nodded back. I looked back at the woman. I thought she was a happy-enough-looking interrogator.

Let's begin by making a note of your personal details, she said as she shuffled a number of the sheets of paper on the desk in front of her. I concurred. That's as good a place as any to begin, I said. Name. Address. Age. That sort of thing. To all of these enquiries I answered truthfully. The woman carried on ticking the relevant boxes with an unnecessarily grandiose sweep of her arm, I thought.

Height?

About…

In centimetres.

Hmm… I'm a feet and inches man, I said. Can you give me a minute?

Weight? Well, it's reducing itself every minute, that's the first thing to take into account, I thought.

I know that, I said.

In kilograms.

Ah… Can you give me a minute?

You're a pounds and inches man, the man chirped up.

Actually I am, I replied.

This job will give you plenty of time to get to know yourself a little bit better, he said.

That's exactly what I've been looking for, I replied, almost with disdain. You see, up until this minor exchange I had thought him her assistant.

Marital status?

I have no one at home, I replied.

Good. This coming from the man again, which might have alerted me to the fact all was not as it seemed. I was only irritated by his interruptions though and thought nothing more about it.

I was asked if I enjoyed my own company. Yes, I said, and it was stressed that I would need to be precise in my work and was that something I considered possible with the personality I had been given? Yes and yes, I said precisely.

Bearing this in mind, the man asked, respond to this poser as truthfully as you can.

Poser?

If you were employed to take the minutes of your meeting with me... he began.

If I was employed? Yes.

With full pension and holiday entitlements, the woman added.

What, by you? I asked.

I beg your pardon?

If I was employed by you?

It doesn't matter in this imaginary scenario who you are employed by, the man replied.

I see.

And a third person were to come to you following the conclusion of said meeting and tell you that you were mistaken in what you thought you'd heard me say... by the way, how is your hearing?

Very good, I said.

Would you listen to the third person, he asked, or stick to your own interpretation?

Who is the third person?

What?

Who's the third person?

That isn't what I'm asking you.

It doesn't matter who it is, said the woman.

Just answer the question based on the information you have been given, the man reiterated. I turned to the woman.

Are you the third person? I asked her.

You can't answer?

Did you say interpretation?

Yes, said the man.

Isn't that the wrong word? I mean to begin with... The man turned and looked at the woman, who was scribbling notes on my file. She turned the sheet of paper over, slowly looking up when she realised we had stopped talking.

Is it a trick question? I enquired.

Let me put the question to you another way, the woman said, but the man interrupted her: Just answer the fucking question! he barked.

I would have to leave it blank, I said.

What?

If I told you to think about it in terms of the questions we've already asked you, the woman suggested.

About the third person?

Think laterally, said the woman.

Can I get back to you with that? I asked.

The man cursed at me, under his breath.

I'm having problems with the word interpretation, I said. In terms of taking minutes I mean, that would seem to be the wrong word... The man was smiling all of a sudden. Clearly I had managed, with all my flapping about, to hit the proverbial nail on the head.

After the woman had expounded further on the virtues of work and the nature of exactitude, he told me I'd been given the job. This was the biggest surprise yet. As I said, I thought he, who I discovered was called Mr Gatt, was the subsidiary partner of the two. Also I was sure the interview had gone badly, despite all the positive thinking I had applied to it in advance.

During the course of this initial conversation neither of them mentioned my qualifications, or any of the failings I thought had been cruelly exposed during the interview's exchanges.

The woman turned to look at him. She was wondering if he had gone out of his mind. It was the first time she'd acknowledged him since I'd been in the room. He refused to return her gaze and fixed me with a half-smile, which I returned with 25 per cent interest: I mean I attempted the more difficult three-quarter smile. The woman turned her attention back to me.

Congratulations, she said through gritted teeth and with a smile that involved such a low degree of difficulty, in regard to the percentage of smile in it, that it almost wasn't worth scoring; in fact it would have been unrecognisable as a smile in any other circumstance.

I'm happy to be on board, I replied, and I was.

Ms B will fill you in on what you're expected to do, Mr Gatt said.

And I'll pick you up a week next Sunday, at three o'clock. Make sure you're ready.

I was ready. In fact I had never been more ready.

I'd given up the flat and collected all the things I needed into a holdall and a small rucksack; the rest of the stuff I had accumulated over the years I threw into a skip. By the Sunday morning I was sitting with my bags, waiting, by the door.

At precisely three o'clock the intercom sounded, ringing hollowly in the empty flat, sounding unfamiliar to my ears. It was Mr Gatt.

After telling him I'd be straight down, I took a last look around the place. I recalled all the good times before I picked up my bags to leave. When I opened the door Mr Gatt was standing there with his knuckles raised, I thought to strike me. I was surprised so I let out a high-pitched sound, but it was short-lived, I couldn't hold a note like that for more than a few moments. After the cry had petered out we shared a few pleasantries. He walked purposefully over to the window. What a delightful view, he said when he'd arrived there.

I'm not sure about that, I replied.

He's clearly somebody who looks at the half-empty glass and sees it as half-full. I pointed out to him in the desolate landscape below the abattoir, the concrete flats, the concrete playgrounds, the dry riverbed, the bare trees, the black puddles, the railway lines like scars, the gasworks chimneys spewing out smog, the rain cloud sunk in the gutter, the bogs and swamps, the grey roads, the black paths, the dead in rows above and below the ground, the yellow air, the yellow earth, in fact I think yellow was his favourite colour because he was smiling as he looked down on the sorry sight below us. Also, it was looked at through the mist of yellow dirt mixed in with black dust on the outside of the glass, which was something I wasn't easily able to clean. We're eight floors up, I said, as if in explanation.

Delightful, he replied. I don't think he didn't mean it.

I looked up at his face (he was a foot taller than me.) It was a desolate face, like the landscape below. His eyes were black like holes in the ground; at the bottom of each there was a twinkling of what might have been water. Anyway it was enough to animate him. His nose was like two chimney-stacks – is that feasible? His mouth was full of tombstones... and so on.

Surprisingly I wasn't put off. In fact he reminded me of all the male role models I had ever known, rolled into one. He was of an indeterminate age, as all adults are when imagined by children. He wore a short-sleeved shirt. His arms reminded me of my father's arms, which used to pick me up and carry me indoors. He had a five o'clock shadow and it was only just three o'clock.

The city is an exciting place, he said.

Is it?

You have no qualms about leaving it all behind?

We looked at the room. It was of course empty, although I could see the wallpaper was stained where the sofa had originally sat against the wall and the carpet was worn in some places and not in others: the tracks gave away my movements over the years. I felt impelled to point this out to him but he was already moving through to view the other rooms in the flat. I stood and didn't follow him. When he returned I was still standing where he had left me.

No, I said.

What?

I have no regrets leaving this behind, I said.

I like to see where a person has come from, he said to me, because it tells me a lot about the person they might become.

Does it have any bearing on the job?

Not as such, he said. Why, have you got anything to hide?

Nothing, I said. That's the problem.

Is that a problem?

I don't know.

Let's go, he said, after a moment.

Did it tell you anything about me? I asked him as we shuffled out through the door; I let it swing to behind me for the last time.

You are a man who wants to leave his old life behind and find a new and interesting challenge ahead of him, he replied as he pressed the button to call the lift.

I didn't know how to respond to that. I thought later I should have said: You're right, but the lift arrived and of course the moment was lost before the thought had come to me.

As we left the lift on the ground I held the doors for a woman who lived on the floor below me. I had only become acquainted with her when she complained about me walking about in the flat above her. Did she expect me to hover or become a ghost of myself? Anyway she looked right through me. I made no mention of the fact that I would probably never see her again. The doors closed on her, her face set in a frown. When I turned around Mr Gatt had disappeared. I found him waiting for me in the car.

As I approached, the boot opened of its own accord, or it might have been something to do with him, and I dumped my holdall in it. It was a lovely flash car like I said. I ran my hand along the paintwork as I walked round to the passenger side. I climbed in, enjoying the feeling of the cool leather seat under me. He shifted into first gear and pulled away.

We drove out of the city and then along winding country

lanes. Mr Gatt handled the car magnificently I might add, it reacted to his touch without complaint, and the journey was what is commonly described, in motoring terms, as smooth. He also played loud rock music with all the windows wound down. My teeth began to chatter and my head became numb with the cold air. I couldn't wind my window up because he kept his hand on the gear stick, except on tight bends, so that his finger hovered near the controls on the dashboard at all times; on the tight bends, when he clutched the wheel with both hands, I clutched both sides of my seat.

It was dusk when we finally approached the house.

He continued to say nothing. This is how it had been for almost the whole drive. We pulled up and got out of the car. I was glad of the chance to stretch my legs actually.

I became aware of a number of things as I stood there on the side of the road. For a start the air was warmer, being stiller. It was also already darker than I was accustomed to it being. Finally it was silent, save for the ticking over of the engine as it cooled down. He gave me my holdall from the boot and, dropping his keys into the side pocket of his sports jacket, he gestured at me, moving his arm, with the hand on the end of it empty and open-palmed, in a sweeping gesture as if he was introducing me to the house. Then before I saw him move I discovered him already bent over at the door; he had lifted the bunch of keys from his pocket as if by sleight of hand and was turning the key in the lock.

The tour of the house he gave me after that was brief to say the least; he said he had to get back, his wife was sitting at home waiting for him, he presumed she was sitting, with her best dress on, they were going to the opera.

This is the dining room the sitting room the master bedroom your bedroom the study. The toilet and bathroom speak for themselves, he said, as we moved apace from room to room. This is the kitchen and the view out of the kitchen window of the fields; you'll wait until morning for that, when it's light. The cellar door is here off the kitchen. That was the sort of thing he came out with, and then he reiterated that he had to be on his way, telling me again as he was leaving the house that he'd be back before the month was out, exactly as had been discussed when the contact had been signed. Okay, I said as I followed him out into the yard.

When he reached his car I thought he would leave quickly, but he didn't, he went on to tell me something about the history of the nearby town. He pointed, his arm parallel to the horizontal. I was on the other side of the wall, in the yard, looking at him standing behind his car, so I could only see the top half of him. I looked to where he was pointing but it was mainly only darkness; here and there perhaps I could make out a ghostly outline.

The road here, he said, leads into the town and links it to the city, the bigger city, where we came from, situated south of here, and to indicate this he suddenly threw out his other arm, his left arm that is, in the opposite direction, so that he looked as if he had been hung out to dry. By now I had inched my way to the gate to get a better view of him, in case he decided to bring any of his other limbs into play, but he only lowered his left arm before suddenly highering his right, so that it was now at about 45 degrees from the horizontal.

If you walk east from here, he said, the land begins to rise and then curve north, to run, in fact, as a modest ridge, all the way up the eastern edge of the town. The town was a tiny settlement before the arrival of peoples from the north signalled an extensive twenty-year building programme. Originally they chose the site because they thought it was on an impregnable flat plain at the foot of the ridge.

If you want to get up there, he said, referring to the ridge, follow the road, and as soon as it is possible, having passed beyond the bushes and ditches that prevent it, make your way into the fields and walk straight ahead; keep the hedgerow within reach on your right and you won't go far wrong. And from up there, he said, raising his arm still further, you'll get a sense of the whole lie of the land.

The local population rose more than a thousand-fold almost overnight, he said, as the town effectively became a dormitory town for the ever-expanding city to the south. Within a few years the civil servants that had settled in the housing estate developments that had been constructed around the perimeter of the original settlement demanded their own autonomy and introduced the idea of a greenbelt to prevent the city swallowing up the town completely. The families of the original settlers began to die out. And the new founding fathers immediately looked to have a Town Council of their own, which was in itself a declaration of intent.

You'll see from up on the ridge how the town is constricted by the greenbelt, Mr Gatt said. You'll see a few houses leaking over the border along the only road out of town, built before ribbon development was identified and stamped out, and here, the very last house, he said, nodding over my shoulder, which existed before the road was even built. I was impelled to turn around momentarily.

You'll also see that the greenbelt is exactly that, he added, a circular tract of land that surrounds the town like a moat. I considered this for a moment.

The ridge protects the community against marauders from the east, he said, and the sea is only a few miles away, due west and north-west of the town, there's comfort in knowing that also. Again he adjusted his pointing arm so that it pointed I supposed due west and he swept it in a shallow arc, in what I presumed was a northerly direction.

You will have deduced, therefore, he said, that the only recognisable threat comes from the unprotected south.

He opened the car door and stood, one foot, his right, in the well in front of the driving seat while the other was still standing on the road: with his left hand he gripped the roof of the car while holding open the car door with his right. Then he said, and his tone was now more intimate: If I had the choice I wouldn't go to the opera, but the wife is a fan.

I nodded.

I'd stay here and we could have a drink, he said.

I nodded again. We both stood still for a moment considering the possibilities that might have been open to us if his wife hadn't been such a big fan of the opera. He looked as if he was enjoying himself more than I was.

What time is it? he finally asked himself, pulling the sleeve back on his left wrist with his right hand to have a look at his watch, and while he was doing this, hands-free, his right foot still in the well in front of the driving seat, I realised everything was dependent on his left leg, which was still standing on the road; any kind of minor mishap and he was on his arse, I thought.

Too late for any of that, he said soberly and I suppose in reference to the wild time he was having in his imagination with all the possibilities. He ducked suddenly out of sight, disappearing into the darkness of the luxury car. A second later the rock music started up again, mid-song, before it was immediately muffled when the door slammed shut; soon it would fade away into the night completely. He revved the engine a few times and before he pulled away he flicked on the headlights. It was at that moment I first saw the woman. She had appeared in front of the car as if from nowhere and now stood in the full beam of the lamps. Mr Gatt honked on his horn twice but the woman didn't move, so he revved the car threateningly at her. She remained adamantly motionless. Finally he stuck his head out of the window and shouted out over the loud rock music: Get out of the fucking road, you stupid bitch! She wouldn't move though, not until he relented, and by the time he finally turned off the engine and opened his door she was already moving around to meet him. Pointing at me she said: Who's that?

Mr Gatt got out of the car, all his limbs appearing almost at once, tight together to begin with and as soon as they cleared the restrictions of the door frame they exploded outwards. He towered over her, at least for now, while he was in this rage, and he bellowed: What the fuck do you think you're doing?

Who's that? She was unfazed by his anger, which was anyhow quickly dissipating.

You know very well who it is, he said. What did I tell you?

Meanwhile I was standing by awaiting an introduction.

I told you I didn't need anybody, she said.

I don't care. I tell you who and what you need, he said, to which she visibly stiffened. Your reports are not subjective when I leave you to your own devices. She began to flap at the mouth, lost for words or finding the words she had available to her to be ineffectual. So she turned on her heel and walked defiantly past me into the house. After a moment Mr Gatt turned to me and smiled.

That's Mona, he said, and that was that. Of course I'd already been told a little bit about Mona, but nothing to prepare me for this.

Don't leave me on my own with her, I said, but I was helpless.

He got back into his car and left.

When he was out of sight I turned round. The house was a collection of lighted windows: he'd turned them all on when he rushed me from room to room. I couldn't get any more sense of the exterior of the house, or the grounds around it, because of the darkness. I hesitated. Then one by one, as I stood there, the lights went out.

I went back inside.

I took my bag into the bedroom and unpacked my things straight away. The clothes I had brought with me I put in the wardrobe, my toothbrush and soap I took into the bathroom. On the way back to my room I stood on the landing outside the master bedroom. On the door was a hand-drawn sign that read: Mona's room. Keep OUT! The sign looked as if it had been coloured in by a child.

This is how it works. I share the house with Mona, although in truth she is hardly ever here, and when she is she doesn't give me the time of day. She too comes as part of the job, although she is one step further up the hierarchical ladder then I am; you'll see she thinks about that a lot by her superior attitude.

It's Mona's job to bring cassette tapes back to the house and leave them with me; in fact she leaves them on the corner of the desk in the study so that she doesn't even have to bother talking to me. Sometimes she comes and goes in the night, when I'm asleep.

Every morning I enter the study, and if there are tapes on the desk, new tapes left in the night, or tapes that I didn't finish with the day before, it's my job to sit down with a pad and pen, listen through my headphones and write down all the things recorded onto them, word for word. That's what I do, I exactly transcribe the recorded conversations Mona has overheard in the town and the occasional description, added in her own voice, of what she has seen, to accompany the conversations and give them some context.

The tapes I have been listening to feature conversations between a man and a woman who appear to be at the heart of everything, although I don't think they are fully aware of their importance.

I have no names for the two voices, so have called them Jack and Jill after the Jack and Jill who went up the hill, to personalise them. On the pad in front of me I refer to them as X for her and Y for him, a clever reference to their chromosomal proclivities, I thought.

Him I imagine as a thickset man because of the deep timbre of his voice and her as a stick-like woman mainly because it amuses me to see the two of them together.

They seem to be involved in some sort of covert activity, the importance of which cannot be under- or overestimated, while a whole cottage industry of espionage exists in their wake, which somebody surely sits at the pinnacle of. The beautiful irony is that Mona is more than likely a spy herself, at least that's the explanation I like best: she is spying on the spies. Mona has been able to gain access to the most sensitive areas of local government, such as it is, although how she has done this I have not been made a party to. And while everyone understandably concentrates their attention on this person at the top of the pile, I exist anonymously at the bottom. I collate information and I am happy to do it, I have never been encouraged to add anything to the dialogue, which I am pleased about; in fact it is clearly stipulated in my contract that I only transcribe, which suits me down to the ground. For me there is no opportunity for intrigue or imagination, and there is no leg up for it either.

Sometimes Mona might also give her opinions on the tapes, which I don't have to agree or disagree with because it isn't my job to have an opinion of my own, although it's easy to see how I might be convinced by any of the many different interpretations of events Mona throws up on the tapes, but it's not my job to offer an opinion on Mona's opinion or on anyone else's opinions for that matter. I'm not sure it's Mona's job to have an opinion either; her opinions incidentally are of negligible importance and never intrude into the ongoing dialogue, I mean. She never speaks in the snippets of conversation she records.

Sometimes I imagine, to spice the job up a bit, that Mona is directing her opinions at me, and not at the person who receives my transcripts after I have finished with them. (And there must be a person after me, who somehow uses the information I have transcribed to some end, or I am doing it for nothing, and where would be the point in that? I am not even at the end of the line then. I realise I am like the last station through which the train passes, always without incident, on its way to the terminal.)

When the transcripts are ready, I am assured Mr Gatt will turn up in his luxury car to collect them.

There are many positive aspects to this arrangement. For one I have managed to avoid responsibility at last, which is a good thing in my view, because I do not respond very well to responsibility, I know that much about myself, even though I have always attracted it. Every position I have held in the past has started like this, with me at the very bottom, but I always rise through the ranks and am suddenly running the business, I can't seem to help myself. I unconsciously present a demeanour telling the people in power, whom we rarely see, that I am a man of finite emotional resources, which is attractive to them; they can then better manage and mould me in their image. But at the same time I also maintain a posture suggesting I possess the strength to survive if not prosper under their rule, which pampers, if not consciously, to their desire to maintain the status quo, I might be seen to be both progressive and reactionary. Little do they know though, my strength is granted to me in short bursts and soon enough I always find myself battered between the orders of those managing me from above and the needs of those I manage, under me. I am caught up in a desperate situation, a struggle to function above and beyond my limitations, which are hidden, and as the gap between the two, their expectations and my limitations, widens, I lash out, usually against myself. Invariably the whole thing ends very badly.

The difference I see with this job is that I am well and truly out of the way. I can't hope to impress my superiors when I have no contact with them, when I do not really know who they are even. I am simply a cog in the wheel and I have no influence on how quickly the wheel turns, or in what direction.

I believe I have found my place in the world.

Jack and Jill have become my only company, since I have been avoiding Mona. I spend a lot of time in my room considering my position, which seems to me to be far less desirable now than it seemed to me to be before, when the idea of coming here was still only an idea. I'd imagined I'd be alone of course and I'd set about my task diligently and methodically.

I remembered again and again the moment when Mona reared up like a monster in the car headlights.

Because I never left my room I also ate next to nothing. Subsequently my body began to act against me as well. I thought

I had gone to the kitchen late one night and found it sitting at the table with Mona, stuffing itself with potted meat sandwiches and plotting my downfall. I awoke suffering from hunger pains, but was aware it might have been my body playing tricks on me. We came to some sort of compromise: I raided the fridge, slicing cheese so thin I could see through it, and retreated to my room with it between two slices of dry bread.

I got to know my room very well during that time. It seemed to me to be exactly square. There was a single cot bed in it, a wardrobe, an office stool and a table in the corner, which had become cluttered because there was no other surface to put anything down on. A squat wicker chair was placed by the window, looking out onto the terrace and the yard. I could see approximately 400 yards down the road both to the left and to the right. Sometimes I watched cars and occasionally the odd person passing the gate, every one of them, without exception, taking a moment to examine the house for any sign of life.

There were thin blue curtains hanging at the window and a circular patterned rug on the bare board floor. Otherwise the room was free of any ostentation, there were no ornaments to speak of.

When the small supply of food I had requisitioned to my room ran out I planned sorties to the kitchen; I was very light on my feet for a heavy man, and my jaunts passed without incident. And they continued until I went out into the yard on the fourth morning; I had opened the door to bring in the groceries and was enticed outside by the sun. I deduced it had hardly rained because all the bushes and trees had a slightly brown tinge to them and we were still well ahead of autumn.

I looked back at the house. It was as if I was seeing it for the first time. It was much older and larger than was suggested by its interior. The impression I'd formed of it from my imprisonment inside was in almost direct opposition to the expectations you might have of it if approaching it from the road. Inside it had the look of a modern home, all the walls being square to one another and flat; there were none of the bumps that you might find in an older house, where the electric wiring runs closer to the surface. It had a fitted kitchen and fitted grey carpets throughout the downstairs. In fact everything that could be fitted was fitted. All the lights were on dimmer switches. The bathroom had a new suite, a basic shower and a heated towel rail. The house was centrally heated throughout. The ceilings were the standard recommended distance from the floors, lower than used to be the norm.

I considered now its finer points, visible to me from the outside. It was made of what I presumed was the local stone. It seemed to sit slightly forward on its haunches so that its rear end appeared to be raised up, that is, the ground below the kitchen window would come up to the knee of anyone standing on a level with the foundations at the front of the house. In truth the building sat quite square, it was the field that was doing the encroaching, it was slowly engulfing the house. If nobody embarked on digging the house out, I thought, in less than a million years (by my rough calculations) the house would be underground.

The windows from the outside looked to be perfectly placed, when they seemed, on the inside, to be fitted high up on the walls. I realised the ceilings had been lowered, creating dozens of unused spaces deep inside and dotted about the house, between the floors of the upstairs rooms and the ceilings of the rooms below them. It was like I was seeing everything for the first time, as I said, and I want to be clear about the next realisation I had. My considering afresh my perceptions of the property also caused me to subconsciously reassess my opinions of Mona. I'd built her up into something monstrous, but now I was able to think about the smaller kernel within her that was probably the real Mona, the heart of her that was un-doubtedly riddled with insecurities. I smiled when I imagined her lack of confidence. I looked at her brusque attitude as a failing and failings are very much more attractive to a man like me, with failings of his own. I thought if I can't help her at least I might for a moment feel superior.

The day was made all the more pleasant because of this revelation and I stood in the yard until the warm feeling had started to run out of me. I looked at the house again in the hope it might be prolonged. While I was waiting I decided to stand my ground in my forthcoming encounters with Mona.

Mona turned up during my tea break. The first thing you'll notice about her is that she has one eye higher than the other. She is conscious of this and attempts to hide it by wearing the eyebrow of her other eye, the lower eye, arched, as if this will level things out, but it only adds a further lopsidedness to her features, a further sense of up and down, and it gives the impression that she is always knowingly surprised. My first words to her are almost always spoken in self-defence.

I'm on my tea break, I said, in answer to what I thought was a disparaging look from her, but it might not have been. She walked straight through the sitting room, without answering me, into the kitchen. Actually something looked different about her today, I thought, so I got up and followed her. She stood leaning against the kitchen work surface waiting for the kettle to boil.

What's the matter, I asked.

Will you stop asking me that? You ask me that every time you see me.

Do I? I asked, a little taken aback. Did I? I did. Now it had been pointed out to me I realised I did, but I couldn't help it. After you notice her one eye higher than the other, the second thing you notice about her is that she always seems troubled in some way, or sad. Anyway I always want to ask her, after I've noticed she looks troubled, or sad, and I've asked her if she's all right, is if she hasn't got the wrong impression about me. Instead I asked: Have you got any new tapes for me?

No, she said, disparagingly. Have you finished the ones I gave you yesterday?

I retreated to the study and sat down at the desk. Before I did anything else I counted almost on one hand all the minutes I had spent in the same room as Mona since I had arrived. My tactics had had little success. She responded to my new approach by trying to make me feel uncomfortable. She said little or nothing, but approached any task aggressively. Preparing food, she would strike the oven with the pan or the table with the plate. I remained impassive and unmoved. I performed the same tasks with even more diligent attention than previously, in order to accentuate further the ridiculousness of her posture. Anyway she soon abandoned this strategy, preferring to stay out of the house altogether, returning when I was asleep and leaving before I was awake. The only sign she had been there at all were the tapes she left behind.

I wondered if perhaps there were some clues as to the reason for her nasty personality traits on the tape I had begun transcribing that morning. I put the headphones back on. So far Jack and Jill hadn't been speaking about anything in particular, only comings and goings, the usual, as if Mona had sat with them over their morning coffee, listening in on their inane small-talk. If any of this was up to me I wouldn't bother recording this tittle-tattle at all, but Mr Gatt had assured me the truth is in the details, so I diligently wrote it all down.

It was true that over the course of the last couple of weeks the name of the Leader of the Town Council had cropped up a number of times. His wife, who had always been eminent in the company of others, had been seen meeting a mysterious man. Jill was adamant they discover, first of all, the identity of the man, but Jack had already taken the liberty of looking into it. *His name is Mr Wood and he works in the Building Control Department,* he told her. *I have a contact,* he added, *he built my kitchen extension.*

Jack's hypothesis that she might be *'up to no good'* caused a tense pause to open up between them. I looked down at the pad in front of me. The last line I had transcribed read: *I'm only saying it's something worth considering,* which Jack had said.

I turned the tape back on and after a momentary pause Jill responded: *I know what you're trying to say.*

I held the pen over the paper while listening to the silence, which was intermittently broken by the wind blowing across the microphone, or it might have been Mona breathing, yes that was probably it; after all I hadn't imagined this meeting to be outdoors.

Meanwhile I pictured Jill, her coffee cup in her hand, glancing casually left and then right, although she was anything but casual, while Jack, sitting close by, had a smug grin playing across his lips.

I didn't really like Jack. I noticed he had a tendency toward melodrama and this was a fine example of it. I expected Jill to ask him what evidence he had for presuming the Leader of the Town Council's wife was involved in anything untoward, but she said nothing of the sort. There was only the sound of crockery, somebody putting their cup on their saucer, or their cup and saucer on the table. I could hear there were other muted voices in the background. This might be a public place: I imagined the village square, a little café overlooking the war memorial; it isn't that busy at this time in the morning though, Jack and Jill, they're alone except for a couple I imagine in the corner who're too involved in each other to notice what they might be talking about, and a single man perhaps reading a newspaper at the counter.

I take my attention back to the table Jack and Jill are sitting at and then to the waitress, who is walking past it with a pastry and a cup of coffee. She's wearing an apron, which has a pocket in the front to keep her pad and pencil in. She's worked here for fifteen years I suppose, ever since she left school and married her childhood sweetheart, whom she's grown less fond of over the years. Or alternatively it might be a young girl and this is her first summer job. Anyway Jack signals to her – by raising his finger in the air – that he would like the bill; that's all he needs to do, the waitress knows him he's here almost every morning with the same woman. She returns to the counter to tot up the figures.

At the moment I can't see Mona anywhere but she must be there because I hear Jack say: *Do you?*

But that's not what you're saying, replies Jill. *You're talking about things being ruled in, not out, because as I said there has been no mention as I said… I just don't want to begin making any rash judgements.*

Then that sounds like Jack coughing into his hand, perhaps he really has a cough.

I'll get it, says Jill; she's talking about the bill I presume, and Jack's coughing to avoid paying it. There follows a flurry of activity as Jill opens her handbag (I can hear the catch) and takes out her purse.

Let him buy his own bloody coffee, I think, as I imagine Jack straightening his tie and brushing the crumbs off his trousers (crumbs?… what crumbs?… maybe he's had a pastry as well…). Jill puts coins on the silver plate and takes the receipt. *Thank you*, says the waitress (yes she's middle-aged, so my first instinct was correct), and she takes the plate away. I'd like to say you can hear all that but I'd be lying – of course I'm filling in the gaps, I'm making all sorts of presumptions. In fact here's another one: by the time Jill has put her purse away in her bag and got to her feet Jack is already on the street outside, she can see him through the window. He's adjusting his trousers at the waist and for a moment it looks like he has his hands on his hips. With his feet apart he might be affecting the classic pose of a superhero. What a prick, Jill thinks. How did I end up in this god-forsaken hole working with a man like this? I smile to myself as Mona follows Jill out. I hear the door open and the sounds from outside suddenly coming in: birds, the occasional car and the chatter of the people around and about, which is different out here, it disperses outwards and upwards, leaving only the slightest trace of itself behind.

The next time I saw Mona she was standing in the yard, sniffing the air. She wasn't aware I was watching her through the sitting room window.

She looked around, but she wasn't looking back at the house, her attention seemed to be focused on the few feet closest to her.

The phone rang, disrupting my reverie. Mona tensed when she heard it and then, turning on her heel, made her way off down the road. The phone's in the hall. I went through to answer it. It was Mr Gatt.

How's things?

Fine.

That's a beautiful part of the world, he said.

It is, I said.

You've been making the most of it?

I have, I lied.

If only I had the time, he said, I'd come down and we could spend a walking weekend together.

When all our small-talk was out of the way he wanted to speak to Mona. I told him she wasn't in.

She's not in, the bitch.

I don't know where she is, I replied, she doesn't tell me where she's going or when she'll be back.

She's a very private person, he offered. You mustn't take it personally.

She isn't warm and considerate like I was led to believe she would be, I said.

She's warm and considerate all right, he replied, somewhat miffed. I've often been party to her warmth and consideration at first hand, but it's something that has to be teased out of her.

Well…

What sort of a man are you anyway? he wondered. You have to work at it.

I wondered out loud how hard I'd have to work.

You're not afraid of hard work?

I'm not afraid of hard work, no, I said, but it isn't only that. She's determined. I should have suspected something from the off.

Well, we were all hoping for the best, he said in reply. When I met you I thought the two of you might be able to get on.

Don't get me wrong, I said.

Work at it, he said again.

I'm not saying it's impossible.

If there's one piece of advice I might offer you, he said.

Yes?

Work at it.

That's what I wanted to say, I replied. I don't want you to think I'm not the man for the job.

She's just pissed off. She fancies herself as a one-woman band. Give her some time and she'll come round.

I'm sure, I said.

Count on it, he said. Count on it. And in the meantime continue to enjoy the fresh air and the exercise. He told me to expect him on Friday afternoon. Make sure you're ready, he said. When I'd put the phone down I wondered what I had to be ready for.

I found new tapes on the corner of the desk in the study. I went into the kitchen to have some coffee before getting started on them. Mona was sitting at the table in her coat, a cup of tea warming her hands. She looked a little sad.

Is everything all right? I asked her, to which she only cocked me a sideways glance; her other eyebrow, the one over the higher eye, arched too, causing her face to fall into disarray. That's a good sign, I thought.

Then she said: There's tea in the pot.

I poured myself a cup and sat opposite her, our knees almost touching, at the scarred wooden table; I always noticed the crosshatches someone had carved along one edge of it, as if counting the days until getting out of here.

Meanwhile Mona was staring into space.

I thought you were out, I said. She didn't reply. I allowed my mind to wander too. By the way, I thought, what could I see over her shoulder? The sun was out, I noticed through the small window over the sink. There was dirty crockery in the washing-up bowl; she must have been hungry when she came in.

You've still got your coat on, I told her, as if she didn't know.

I'm on my way out, she said.

Haven't you just come in?

Yes, she said, but I've got to go out again.

I had the feeling there was something she wanted to tell me, probably nothing about Jack or Jill, but perhaps stories from her life before this one. There might be nothing in my past I thought worth talking about but it occurred to me we might find some neutral ground if we could talk about what she did before she came here. She might have a family. I was reminded of the childish sign on her bedroom door. Maybe her child has to sit some more exams. I didn't know how to get her started though because I'm on my own here all of the time and I've forgotten how to interact with other people; I'm sure I could ask for groceries or tell somebody the time in the street, but I could straight away tell this was something different; for a start something might have been expected of me.

She told me she had heard a noise in the night. So that was it. This was the first line of a rare conversation between us, so I lapped it up.

What did she mean, I asked her, was it a person she could hear, or an animal in the yard? I posited it might have been any kind of animal. I wanted to tell her I had seen some terrible animals through the kitchen window stalking the perimeters of the property and then, although she might have hated me for a moment as the bringer of bad tidings, she would probably turn to me for some sort of comfort. Anyway she didn't know whether it was an animal or a man.

I haven't heard anything, I said to her, unable to do anything but tell the truth in the end.

She wanted to know how I slept. Fine. I do. On my back, I said. I hardly ever wake up. She's up most of the night, she told me. It's a vicious circle. She can't settle so she gets up and has a glass of water and a cigarette, of course that doesn't make her feel like going to sleep; the glass of water has made her want to pee and she feels like she ought to brush her teeth again because the cigarette has left a nasty taste in her mouth. Anyway she's surprised her moving about hasn't woken me. Nothing wakes me, I said, someone could kill me in my sleep and it wouldn't wake me. She didn't see the funny side so I didn't push it. To be honest I thought she was imagining the noises, although I didn't tell her this. She's just not used to the sounds of the countryside, any more than I am. She's tired so she's susceptible to suggestion. I asked her how long she'd been here. Maybe she's been here a lot longer than I think and is used to the noises and knows when they contain some kind of threat. I mentioned Jack and Jill's investigation into the Leader of the Town Council to change the subject, but she didn't flinch.

If she knew anything more about it, or has any kind of opinion, she wasn't giving it away. I was just trying to take her mind off the subject of the noises, I told her. I have a few thoughts on the subject myself. Anyway it didn't necessarily follow that she would know any more than I did anyway. The main thing was she was talking to me now at least.

Her eyes settled on me, but it was only every now and then I was in focus; I also saw her look beyond me, then at another moment settling her concentration on the lip of the mug she was holding between us and between her hands, her elbows resting on the table. I looked at her for quite a while before I was surprised all of a sudden by a desire to kiss her. I don't know why I should be surprised; actually I think it was probably because she was a woman. I have a similar longing for most of the woman I meet and I even have feelings for Jill, whom I have never seen and who is mostly made up by me. Although I knew it might only be a momentary feeling, I also knew it'd keep on coming back now that I'd had it once. I have first-hand knowledge of feelings like these and I know they've been here before, regularly, and they always come back. Someone just needs put a woman in front of me, and once I've had that feeling about her it'll keep on coming back until the woman is taken away and a new one is put in front of me in her place.

I took a sip of the tea; while I'd been warming up, having the desiring thoughts about Mona, the tea had started to go cold. I was happy of the distraction. The moment when I might have said something to Mona had gone, along with the terrible pictures that had been running like a film in my head of what would happen if I'd acted on the impulse. Nevertheless when she got to her feet I couldn't stop myself from thinking: she's a fine figure of a woman when she's in a vertical position.

Anyway, for me, the ice felt like it had finally been broken, or there was a crack in it at least. She said: I'll see you later, which widened the crack, before she walked out. Yes, I said and then, very urgently I added, plunging the both of us into the freezing waters (which caused my voice to rise in pitch): Please take care! This last-gasp comment got a startled little look from her, over her shoulder. It wasn't enough to stop her though, and her momentum carried her through the door. I saw her head as it passed the kitchen window, with her face on the side of it that was turned to look in through the glass, and her mouth was slightly agape and both her eyebrows were going up and down like the clappers. She might have managed to brake just out of sight, I thought, and there, at a standstill, spent a moment wondering at the heartfelt sentiment that I had saturated my last words with, just as I'd wanted her to, but she probably thought it misplaced, as it might have been, I couldn't be sure. Anyway I decided not to get to my feet and go to the window to check just in case I saw her striding off across the fields, unaffected, or the opposite: she might be standing there, her heart quickened, probably her mind in confusion, looking back at me, which would be worse.

I thought: What am I trying to do? Do I have any feelings for Mona, or am I just lonely? I decided to have a think about it when I had calmed down, maybe during my tea break, but I couldn't help having a little think about it now, as I walked into the study, and this is what I thought: I thought I do have feelings for Mona but they are skewed – in some way I couldn't yet figure out – by my solitude. How would we get on if she spent any real time in the house with me? Then I started to think about the dirty cup she had left on the kitchen table and the dirty pots she had left in the sink, and that's all I had time to think, because I was trying to put it out of my mind.

When I was in the study I saw the tapes waiting for me on the corner of the desk. They sat there, tantalisingly, in view of the new intimacy I had shared with Mona, and because they were from a time previous to its having manifested itself. I imagined how her tone might differ with me on any future recordings. Would she load her voice with hidden inflections? I make it part of my job to search out even the tiniest of nuances in a person's voice. Then suddenly I thought: Mona is out there in the world, and for the first time it occurred to me that she might be in danger. I was able to take my mind off her plight though by sitting down and putting on the headphones; this always took me into another world altogether.

The first tape I put in the machine I had to rewind, and I looked at the pictures tacked up on the wall over the desk as

I listened to the purr of the mechanism, working and audible in my headphones.

They had been here since before I came, I mean I didn't put any of them up. One was a photograph of the vista from the road outside the house. I could see the recognisable fields and the trees and that the sky was blue across the top but I couldn't see the derelict barn over to the right, because it had landed out of shot. Also there was no sense of this as greenbelt land, on either side of it houses. It looked in the photograph as if it was the country and nothing but the country. Another picture next to it showed a woman standing in front of a mosaic wall of some sort. She looked uncomfortable. Her jerkin was zipped up tight to her chin as if it was all that was holding her head up. And like the head, supported by the collar, the wall was held up by a mesh fence; it looked as if it was ready to fall down without it. Maybe the woman was uncomfortable because of the precariousness of the wall she was standing in front of, especially now she had her back to it. She was bravely attempting a smile nevertheless, so I was able to assume the blood necessary to work the muscles was still getting to the head, despite the tightness of the collar.

I wondered who the woman was, as I did every morning when I sat down at the desk. I saw through her smile. It was a grimace carefully plastered over. On most days I would create a short 250-word or so fantasy about her while I was waiting for the tape to rewind but today, before I could picture her in a picturesque setting, which I always preferred, I realised I was distracted by thoughts of Mona again and of other thoughts trying to keep the thoughts of Mona at bay. There is no precedent, I had been thinking, for love at first sight in my life, although of course it wasn't love at first sight for Mona and myself either, my feelings were the result of my having been starved of all human contact. That called into question the validity of the feelings surely.

That woman in the photograph might have been Mona, I decided, except it didn't look like her. What's the point in thinking about Mona anyway, I thought, did she remind me of any of the other women I had suffered relationships with? People say everyone has a type. Was Mona my type? I wasn't sure what my type was. In the heat of battle I always succumbed to a woman with a strong personality, and from this point on the roles were set. This though wasn't what I would have liked for myself, it had merely become the norm. Now I am aware of it, I thought, in the future I can make sure to avoid it; I decided to look for a woman whom I could subjugate to my will for a change.

There was the click of the tape machine as the rewinding came to a halt. I thought about where we all were, Jack and Jill, Mona watching them, and me in the study listening in.

Jack it seemed had rediscovered his previous convictions: he spoke about the Leader of the Town Council's wife and her liaisons with Mr Wood, describing them as *'illicit meetings'*, as if he were accusing her of murder.

Jill was not willing to entertain accusations of impropriety without proof though. So nothing new.

Meanwhile Jack's contact, from the Minor Works Project Design and Management Services in the Building Control Department, had suggested a meeting with a man he knew from the Strategic Planning and Investment Team, a Mr Scrivener.

Mona reported on the day of the meeting that Jack and Jill met in their usual café and then abandoned it for The Tea Rooms on the other side of town. I found myself imagining Jack and Jill decamping from one café to the other; it's true, from what I had gathered, the place they always breakfasted in wasn't anything to write home about. (Did Mona mention that or was it something I just made up?) Anyhow I imagine Jack, the picky sod, standing up suddenly in the café and complaining about the lack of preserves to spread on his croissant. Jill is probably sitting there, happy with her cinnamon swirl (and who wouldn't be?), looking around. She's mortified (what's he doing?), maybe she even catches Mona's eye, but she doesn't know whom she's looking at, and, not having anything else to communicate to each other, they both look again at Jack, whose head they see has filled up with blood. I'm not sure Jack should be doing this actually, isn't his red head attracting attention, which is surely the last thing they want? I don't care though. I leave him to it. Maybe Jill is trying to draw Jack's attention to this oversight, she's waving her spoon with the coffee froth already crusted onto it in the air, but he's too angry about the jam to be able to see anything else clearly; everybody is getting the chance to watch him gesticulating and generally making a tit of himself though, until Jill hisses through her teeth: Sit down! Jack turns to look at her, already he has his curses all lined up – fuck you, fuck them, and so on – but then everything about the situation suddenly dawns on him, at last, as the red mist subsides, as the blood runs out of his head. He half-heartedly lifts his hand in the air as he takes his seat, never mind what he means by it. He finds himself blushing: the blood having performed an about-turn then in order to fill up his cheeks again, only this time it's using different vessels. Jill looks at the curl of pastry on the plate in front of her rather than have to look at him. She probably says, almost under her breath: Let's get out of here.

Mona, of course, would have been somewhere in the room, taking note of all this, although she makes only a passing reference to it. As a scene it wouldn't do much for Jack's reputation in her eyes.

I find out soon enough of course their flit had nothing at all to do with jam, it was Mr Scrivener who had expressed a preference for meeting in The Tea Rooms, away from the prying ears of Town Council colleagues who frequented the usual café.

So they decamp across town as a threesome, a two-person frontline with Mona following up. Jack and Jill think they are just the two of them, maybe they think the imminent arrival of the man from the Strategic Planning and Investment Team makes him the third person.

Mr Scrivener is waiting for them when they arrive. The voices of Jack and Jill become somewhat inaudible amongst the clatter of cups and background chatter, except I hear a few hellos and other words of introduction.

No, over here, I hear Mona say, in response to a waiter showing her to a table away from Jack and Jill. He mumbles some kind of assent and I hear the screech of the chair legs on lino as Mona makes herself comfortable.

A menu, the waiter says and Mona thanks him. *Pompous fool,* she adds as he probably makes his way away between the tables.

Are you listening? she adds quietly. After a moment I stopped the tape. What did she say? It occurred to me she wasn't talking to the waiter. I rewound the tape and listened to her aside again. There was no response forthcoming from the waiter, which would signify he hadn't heard her. I listened again and again to the insult until I began to discern in it a tone of familiarity.

Impulsively maybe, I decided she was talking to me. I crossed out, on my pad, the sentence, which had already been transcribed. It felt like an act of defiance. The black mark was immediately prominent on an otherwise unsoiled transcript. I stared at it until it seemed to engulf my whole consciousness, manifesting itself as a wave of panic that almost overcame me. The fact is it was now a permanent addition, and a confession, not of ineptitude necessarily, but of a decision made consciously to strike through what had been recorded, noted and deemed therefore sacrosanct. So I had struck the sentence out. What did that mean, or appear to mean?

I turn the tape back on. Mona has chosen a table near enough for me to hear Jack and Jill's conversation with Mr Scrivener. They are talking already.

So how do you know Mr Ledger? Jack asks.

I'm sorry?

I imagine Mr Scrivener as he sits opposite Jack and Jill. The Town Council policy document he had been carrying under his arm is on the table between them. He has a clipped pencil-thin moustache maybe, wavy hair parted and lying flat to his head following years of diligent work with hair wax and a constant battle with overruling nature; even now a few strands have loosed themselves from the grease to reach up toward the sun. On occasion he might take his comb out of his back pocket and set it, with unnerving accuracy, in his centre parting.

He's a fine man, says Jack, *a very fine man.*

We play golf, says Mr Scrivener.

After an awkward pause Jack scoffs: *Golf? Golf? I don't care much for golf.*

Mr Scrivener turns to look at Jill.

What has Mr Ledger already told you? she asks him. Mr Scrivener is silent for the moment. *He told you the Leader of the*

Town Council's wife has been seen speaking to a man from the Building Control Department, she adds.

But there must be more to it than that. Mr Scrivener speaks disdainfully.

This is what I'd like us to find out.

Mr Ledger wouldn't waste my time with a petty affair, Mr Scrivener adds.

What would you like us to tell you? asks Jack.

I beg your pardon?

What would you be satisfied with?

That's not necessary, says Mr Scrivener.

What isn't?

I don't waste any energy wishing for anything, Mr Scrivener replies, *I respond to events.*

That's what I'm interested in, says Jill.

Can we just get this over with? Jack slaps the table, but without conviction. Mr Scrivener chuckles.

They were seen in a private place.

How can it be a private place if they were seen? Mr Scrivener interlocks his fingers and lays his hands on the policy document on the table in front of him. I imagine this because I sense he is setting himself. He lifts a retractable pencil out of his pocket and depresses the end with purpose.

I think you'd be better off speaking to somebody in the Department for Extra-Marital Affairs, he says, and he looks Jack square in the eye.

I don't know anybody in the Department for Extra-Marital Affairs, says Jack.

I do, and he makes a note of something on the document in front of him.

What are you writing?

Would you like me to have a word? asks Mr Scrivener.

Would you? asks Jack.

A silence breaks out, which is broken only by the sound of the penny dropping. *There isn't a Department for Extra-Marital Affairs,* says Jill.

Mr Scrivener makes another note.

What are you writing about? asks Jack.

I needn't tell you this is to be held in the strictest confidence, Jill says.

My lips are sealed, says Mr Scrivener.

We want to find out if this man from the Building Control Department has got anything to do with the Leader of the Town Council's plans to build a new estate on greenbelt land, Jill says.

Mr Scrivener immediately sits up to attention.

What plan?

I must say I am surprised too. Jack and Jill obviously speak to each other away from Mona's microphone because this is the first I've heard about anything like this.

I knew there was something else going on, Mr Scrivener says.

Before we all get too excited, Jill intercedes, *I should tell you it isn't within the Leader of the Town Council's remit to lead that kind of development.*

He'll bring anybody on board he feels he needs to, replies Jack.

Nevertheless I'd like to stress to Mr Scrivener, says Jill, *that all this is unconfirmed.*

That's why you've brought me on board.

Can you help us? asks Jill.

Let me look into it. Mr Scrivener returns his pencil to its pocket and picks up his policy document. *If what you say is true and the Council Committee find out about this the Leader of the Town Council is going to be for the high jump.*

I imagine they catch a sight of the Leader of the Town Council early on every day, going about his business. Actually I wonder what it's like to live a life like his life, I admit it. I fantasise about it. Only in my daydream the Leader of the Town Council is on the run, his undercover activities have been uncovered and the Town Council Committee have turned up at his house in force, each with an axe to grind. It isn't a surprise to me that they find him out; he isn't the Leader of the Town Council for nothing, he's ahead of them every step of the way, he's already packed a small case and legged it. His wife answers the door and the posse crowd past her into the sitting room. One of them has found himself elevated into the position of leader-in-waiting. In human structures there are leaders all the way down, from top to bottom; in fact if there are only two people in the room one of them is going to lord it over the other. The leader in this instance, such as he is, sits in the Leader of the Town Council's chair. He knows whose chair it is, he's visited the Leader of the Town Council before, he's doing it to make a point. He's reminded also of whose chair it is by the wife of the Leader of the Town Council, but he doesn't move, he won't move; occasionally he might shift as if something is biting him from below but he stays on board, directing those under him, despatching them to the furthest reaches of the house to search for the errant leader whose position he has usurped and whose chair he is sitting in. By the time they've discovered the Leader of the Town Council isn't in the house the Leader of the Town Council's wife has put tea and biscuits on the table for everyone. That's OK, we'll wait, says the man who would be leader, and then we won't miss out on the biscuits, which are my favourite, he thinks. Little does he suspect there are already rumblings of rebellion coming from the other members of the Town Council. They have plans of their own, and they're only waiting for the chance to strike, maybe while the would-be-leader is stuffing himself with shortbread.

At the same time the other thing going on is the Leader of the Town Council's wife is sharing a complicit look with the man from the Building Control Department with whom she is embarking upon an affair; it was because of this he was the first to attach himself to the lynch mob. She can still remember the last time they made love, while he recalls that up until now all the shortbreads belonged to him.

Actually Mona has now started to appear in these daydreams

too, often when I least expect it. She suddenly steps out of the shadows, scantily clad, and tells me my terrible secret is safe with her (what secret? I ask her), before we embrace and things lead on nicely from there.

Of course when I first imagined myself on the run, I didn't consider any of the inconveniences that would come along with a life like this. For example, when Mona wasn't stepping out of the shadows at opportune moments I had to wait for her to come to me. I'll come, she'd say. When? Tonight. Tonight? Are you sure? Yes, she'd promise. Only I'm holed up here, I'd say, I can't come to you. I know exactly where you're holed up, she'd reply, we've been watching you, haven't we, but there's nothing I can do, I've got a lot on. What have you got on? I'd ask her. I'll come as soon as I've put Jack and Jill to bed, she'd say. But you'll come tonight? Yes. You're sure? Listen if you don't give over pestering me I'll bring Jack and Jill with me. I stopped myself. Somehow I had gone down the wrong road and got myself into a situation I didn't want to be in. I decided to start my daydream over again, from scratch. This time I imagined we were standing in the Leader of the Town Council's sitting room, his wife was still holding the plate of biscuits, untouched, in her hand. The would-be leader, who had figured himself promoted, was now lying dead at my feet. Before I could get myself in the right frame of mind though, Mona, who I found was standing next to me, claimed responsibility for his murder. I work for some very nasty people, she said.

She'd killed him, and now, from the look in her eye, I'd say she was coming after me.

Shit.

I ended up in a bad mood because I couldn't follow my fantasies through to a satisfactory conclusion. In every one of them I found myself compromised.

Mona didn't come back that night. I had almost finished transcribing the tapes I had been left with and I had to sit twiddling my thumbs. I drank ten mugs of tea while I sat waiting.

Often I didn't sit actually, mostly I stood at the window with my mug of tea in my hand and looked out into the yard and the road beyond that, which was mostly in darkness. When I was in the kitchen I stood at the sink and looked out onto the fields behind the house. What had passed between Mona and myself during our last meeting was undermined by the passage of time. I struggled to bring to life again the previous intensity I'd felt when I had been sure of myself. It didn't help me to be waiting for her like this.

The next day I woke up and lay in bed for a few minutes listening out for noises in the house. Maybe Mona had returned during the night. The thought took me by surprise. I couldn't hear anything, all the sounds were coming from outside: a bird falling out of a tree, the wind opening the gate to the yard, low clouds scraping the earth.

I decided to take a walk. I was reinvigorated by the idea of a different future with Mona; it had come to me during the night, when my mind was uncluttered by my memories. Now I had given up on their validity I was curiously liberated, so much so I could imagine a life together in a fantasy world completely of my own creation: in it neither of us had to be the people we were and I could forget all that had passed so far between us. It mattered less and less that it was a fantasy world.

I roused my body and told it we were going for a walk. For a while it refused to move. Get your shoes on, I said.

A few hours later I found myself standing in the road a few hundred yards from the house. I felt as if I was waking up after a long sleep. I knew I had been out of consciousness for some time because the sun was low in the sky and the trees cast long shadows across the fields on either side of me. Also my belly was rumbling, in fact I think it might have been the noise of that which roused the rest of me from my comatose state. I couldn't feel it but I could hear it. Anyway my legs had stopped a long time ago and all my other organs had shut down too, except my stomach, which had somehow roused itself, without the help of my mind which was also still alive, turning over and over at the centre of it all like a tyre stuck in the mud: Turn back! Turn back, it was screaming at me.

I sat on the terrace, smoking. The sun was out but it was weak and hung down in the high sky. I had no useful purpose. The moments of my remaining life were disappearing at a speed that was quicker than the minutes that were passing in the day. I had finished with the tapes I had been left with and Mona had still not returned with any new ones. The morning felt inordinately long.

I lit another cigarette and inhaled the smoke, which was at odds with the country air itself. I blew it out as a cloud, which clung together until the greater atmosphere was able to get in amongst it and dilute it into the massive body of itself.

I was cowed by my unconditional capitulation to loneliness because I had imagined solitude would suit me fine. My desire to take a trip into town suggested otherwise, while my failure to make any headway along the road had left me shaken.

For a moment the sun came out in the sky and bathed everything in front of me in a carpet of lucidity, as if flecks of white had been fastidiously painted onto the edges of everything that had previously been there. Momentarily I looked on the world with invigorated senses until the sun went in again behind a cloud, which, when I looked up, I saw was in the shape of a life incessantly closing in on itself.

I got up out of my chair because I couldn't sit still any longer and walked around the circumference of the yard and garden. I was looking for signs of the animal that had been keeping Mona awake at night; it was almost certainly some sort of mythological beast made up of the parts of other animals sewn together into the shape of all of Mona's fears. (I had no idea what any of Mona's fears might look like mind you.) I hoped I would find something though so I could kill it.

After a moment any impetus left me and I stood looking over the wall. Down the road I thought I could see the nearest edges of the town encroaching onto the horizon for the first time.

As I watched, a figure I saw in the distance became Mona as it grew closer. She'd lost some of the purposefulness in her stride; her importance was put into some context no doubt by the acres of green fields, the hedges and the trees, which by far outnumbered her. As she got closer she grew bigger still and I was able to make out her profoundly unhappy face, her mouth twisted down at the edges, her nostrils flared, lines vertical and horizontal gathered on her brow. I wondered what might have happened to her. By the time she arrived, all in one go, everything about her bad mood was in sharp focus.

We stood together in the yard for a moment, in silence. I briefly remembered all the thoughts I had been having about her. Without making it look obvious I quickly cast my mind back to the moment I had last seen her, when she had looked back at me over her shoulder, and I studied the look she had on her face. First of all, I thought, at least there's nothing hostile in it, it certainly had none of the anger I had become accustomed to seeing in her looks. If anything it was the first hint of tenderness in her I had seen so far. That's easy to say with hindsight, I thought, but I might just as easily have been wrong. When I thought about it now, I decided it might simply have been caused by a twinge in her neck.

It quickly became apparent, during the course of the few words we exchanged at the gate, that while I had been watching our relationship developing in the amorous direction I wanted it to, for her nothing had changed. If she remembered our final exchange at all, it had barely dented the protective armour she wore about her emotional person.

This got me wondering how many of my other recent thoughts about Mona depended in fact on how she responded to them in reality, and not on how I had expected her to respond in my fantasies. For example: What if she hadn't been scantily clad when she stepped out of the shadows? What if when I imagined her she'd been wearing an overcoat? Maybe things would have progressed very differently. Did I in fact have the strength of mind to face her down, I wondered, even in my own fantasy, and be sure that when I requested her to, she would open the overcoat and reveal a state of scant-cladding underneath?

It seemed to me that seeing her again now cast the whole erotic fantasy into a different light. Maybe it killed it altogether. Now I could only imagine her scowling again.

We adjourned from the yard to the kitchen. I might as well have been in the sitting room watching the television, I decided, because as usual she was immediately unapproachable. Her absence gave me the opportunity to have thoughts of my own though, and as well as all my ruminations, previously catalogued, which sank back a bit into the background, I had another thought, it being the first mention to myself of a plan that I was going to bring to fruition in the next few minutes as soon as Mona had finished talking. It was out of focus at first, jostling for position as it was with the previous understanding that I could have been watching the television, and the curiosity I suddenly had for what might be on, all of which were elbowed to one side by my conscious realisation that Mona was speaking (I had subconsciously already noted this, an event in itself); anyway I certainly couldn't listen to Mona at the same time as thinking anything else, so I quickly jettisoned all deliberations other than those relating to my plan, which I was able to put to one side in clear view for later consideration, and I concentrated on what Mona was saying. I don't think I'd missed too much. She was complaining about the fact nothing was happening with Jack and Jill and she was clearly frustrated.

What are they up to? I enquired.

That seemed to stop Mona in her tracks.

I thought, I didn't mean to sound flippant, I take this as seriously as the next person.

Mona was deliberate in what she said: If nothing happens soon we're in trouble. Then she turned on the kettle.

What do you mean by that? I asked her.

You'll see, she said, and with that threat hanging in the air she was able to draw me closer in so that I found I was making the tea. She sat at the table as I put a mug in front of her.

Why don't you take your coat off?

I have to go out again, she said, I only came back for clean knickers.

Have you got a tape for me?

She shook her head, and she was clearly upset because she saw only failure in this and her unacceptance of her failure was making things worse.

To make the most of her distress I decided to bring into operation the plan I had formulated earlier, picking it up again from its visible position in my nearby consciousness.

Oh, by the way, I said, and I was going to tell her I'd heard the noise that had been bothering her, and it would have been exactly the right time to strike, I think, except that the phone rang and it went unsaid.

If that's Mr Gatt, Mona said hurriedly, tell him I'm not in.

I answered it.

Put Mona on, Mr Gatt said.

She isn't here, I replied, you've just missed her.

Where's she gone?

She's gone out.

The bastard, he said. When was the last time you saw her?

Just now, I replied.

And how was she?

What do you mean?

She can be a cantankerous bitch, he said, I want to be sure she's on the case.

She's on the case all right, I replied.

I'm coming down on Friday, he said and then he hung up abruptly. When I returned to the kitchen Mona was preparing to leave. I didn't want her to go.

Where are you going?

What did he want? she asked.

Nothing. I don't know. He's coming down on Friday. Are you going to be here to meet him? I wondered out loud.

Something needs to happen, she said, or we're out of a job.

You'll be back then?

I was still intent on the coat I was helping her into, I watched her arm sliding into the sleeve and I was still slowing this down in my mind, so I hardly realised the coat had gone and Mona in it.

With Mona out of my sight I was able to resume my erotic dreams about her. Somehow when I was remembering her this was possible. It was only when she was present in the real world she also put her clothes on in my fantasies.

On the Thursday Mr Gatt walked in on us *in flagrante delicto*. I told him to fuck off and he went into the next room, where he waited for us to finish.

Later on that evening Mr Gatt called to remind me he was going to be with us the following day. I didn't tell him about the dream.

Make up a spare bed on the sofa.

You're stopping the night?

I don't know, he replied. Maybe. The wife is visiting her sister. We might be able to have that drink.

He arrived in the early evening. I heard the tinny sound of rock music before I heard the hum of the car engine and at first I didn't know what it was; it came to me like the voice of a dead relative, a whisper, which at first had no apparent source. I looked around in an attempt to ascertain the direction of its approach. Slowly it gathered volume about it until I could make out the words. Needless to say they fell far short of the profundity I had been expecting, I mean this was not the voice of a spirit or an angel describing perhaps how life might be on the other side, it was a graphic description on the nature of one man's carnal feelings for a woman. You can imagine my disappointment.

So I knew he was coming but I still wasn't ready for him. Nevertheless I walked out into the yard to meet him. He parked the car on the patch of grass down the side of the house.

Come in, he said as he walked past me. We've already had a taster of his impatience, he comes with a government health warning. I followed him back inside. He had a small case with him, which he left for the moment in the hallway. He also had a plastic carrier bag, which contained a bottle. He put it on the kitchen table between us, and for a moment we eyed it, me suspiciously, he with something else in mind, he knew after all what was in it. Armagnac, he said, casually. I hadn't a clue what he was talking about.

It's a bit early for me, I said as I put the kettle on, but he found two tumblers on the draining board and poured out a couple of shots anyhow. He told me he calculated his measures in fingers.

How many fingers is that? I asked.

Two, he said, sticking them up at me. He laughed.

Are we having the drink now? I wondered. He held his glass aloft in reply. The results of a traditional process, he said, distilling white wine grapes found in and around a small number of villages in the south-west region of France.

I see, I said, taking the glass he was holding out to me, even though I had only a second ago in my mind told myself I would decline it. Meanwhile the kettle turned itself off and the unused water began to cool off.

The name goes all the way back to Gallo-Roman days, Mr Gatt continued. The first bottle was brewed in 1411, so they say, and within thirty years they were selling it in the supermarkets. I sniffed it; it didn't smell so bad.

I have a sweet palate, he added. I don't like anything that takes my breath away. What about you?

I'm not keen either, I said.

We sat down. It was clear the drinking had begun. I was soon feeling the ill-effects while Mr Gatt seemed happy to go about the business of getting drunk. The next time he gave himself a refill he also topped up my glass. Drink up, he said.

I took a little sip, no not even that, I poured the stuff against my upper lip, which I kept tight to the rim of the glass. Then I lowered it again, with almost all of what had been in the glass before still in it.

He was watching me intently as if he had found me out but he said nothing.

I wondered if drinking might not be another good weapon to use in my fight against the body. I realised I hadn't thought to keep my lips closed and wondered if it might not have been a tactic used instinctively by the body, knowing as it did that if I consumed too much it would become incapable. Of course this only spurred me on to drink. There followed, at regular intervals, disagreements over the relative pros and cons of the alcoholic consumption, my mind saying it'll free the body of inhibitions, the body arguing in its way that the mind, under the influence of the alcohol, was progressively less able to discern a good idea from a bad one. Some of the battles I won and some of them I lost.

Mr Gatt asked me to give him a summing up of what Mona had been able to find out. I told him, in brief, what had been going on with Jack and Jill. When I'd finished I asked him who they worked for.

He told me, without a moment's hesitation, that they worked for the Town Council. Who did I think they worked for?

I didn't know.

Who do you think I work for?

I don't know that either, I said.

We all work for the Town Council, he replied.

Even me?

Even you, he said.

My department, he told me, was one of many different departments, and everybody, it seemed, who had their own department, more often than not knew nothing about what the other departments were doing.

That's ridiculous, I said.

Maybe so.

Maybe so?

It makes the whole bloody thing difficult to police, he told me. Which is where I come in.

The alcoholic spirits seemed to let loose in him an exuberance previously unseen, whereas they raised in me only the spectre of melancholia I had with me at all times, and which I mostly kept at bay. Slowly my head began to spin, I mean slowly the feeling came upon me, and then the spinning itself began slowly.

Let's presume there's a rumour the Leader of the Town Council is involved in some dodgy property dealings, Mr Gatt said. Who decides he needs to have a tail put on him?

If there's a tail on him, I wondered, wouldn't the Leader of the Town Council need to know about it?

Not necessarily, Mr Gatt said, and he can't keep a tab on what every department is doing.

Unless he creates a new department to do it for him, I suggested.

That's right, Mr Gatt replied. Which would mean bringing in more of the likes of you and I. And all these new You and Is would need a bed to sleep in, he added, and an office to work in. Yes. There simply isn't the room for them, he said. There aren't the funds either, nor the political will to go out looking for them.

The growth of the town, he explained, has given rise to a bigger and more complicated civil service. Sub-committees are set up to police areas the committees decide require less regulation. The result of this, of course, is that more staff are required to man the sub-committees, and this at a time when the public are already ill-at-ease with the size of the civil service as it is. The most radical change to Town Council policy over the last decade has been the creation of a new species called the consultant, which was necessitated, as I said, by both the expanding demand for committees and more recently sub-committees, and the subsequent public outcry at the rate of governmental expansion necessary to cater for the new demand. The consultant is a freelancer, and so remains almost invisible on the register of staff. I am a consultant, Mr Gatt said, and consequently I do not consider myself bound by the rules and regulations prohibiting your general run-of-the-mill civil servant.

There are many things about governmental infrastructure written into our unwritten constitution, he explained, which must remain unwritten.

I started to worry about this statement straight away. If it's only written down on the unwritten constitution I thought, how can I hope to recognise it and obey it as I would a law writ large elsewhere.

The rules and regulations written in the written constitution, he said, by the very fact they are written down are not open to interpretation. This I was aware of, and, as it is, I was already afraid of these laws, and as for the many laws written in the constitution that I remained ignorant of, I was more afraid of them still. Although at least if they're written I thought there might be a chance I would become aware of them at some point. If it's only in the unwritten constitution though, who's to say what it says exactly, and who's to say I wasn't transgressing now? Mr Gatt was clearly a man who was confident about his place in respect of all this.

I became sullen because of the recent realisations, which were making my head hurt, and also because of the drink, which was continuing to affect Mr Gatt in a different way altogether. For a while he became more exuberant still and it was difficult for me to keep up with him. He banged on the table over and over with his glass and opened his mouth without anything coming out when he might have believed he was laying out for me the nature of the universe.

I miss the city, I suddenly said, taking both of us by surprise. He stopped tapping his glass on the tabletop and concentrated on looking at me. I wondered what I might say next.

You live in the city, I said, you must know... and here he interrupted me. I don't want to recall for you any memories of the city, he said, especially if you're starting to miss it. He began to drum quietly, with his fingertips, on the tabletop; if I listened carefully I could distinguish the impact of each of the fingers individually.

I suggest you get yourself into a different frame of mind, he said. None of this should be taking you by surprise.

No, I said.

Because it was stipulated in your contract, we spoke about it during your interview.

I know.

I am not asking you to do anything you didn't sign up to.

Don't get me wrong, I said.

We sat in silence for a moment.

Mona isn't in, I presume, Mr Gatt said. I shook my head.

I know she can be a bit defensive, he said, Mona.

I suppose so, I replied.

You either know what I mean or you don't, he said. She can be a difficult cow.

OK, I said.

Anyhow if she doesn't come back tonight, he said, I'll catch her in the morning. Is that what's bothering you?

I don't know.

He acknowledged nothing was certain in relation to Mona's movements, and he looked around the room as if following Mona's to-ings and fro-ings previous to now and in anticipation of her wanderings in the future. It turned out he was looking around for his bag. I fetched it for him and put it on the floor by the side of his chair, but he never acknowledged it after that. I noticed he had refilled my glass in the meantime, but I didn't touch it; my unsteady journey to retrieve the case had gained some purchase for the body's argument that I had drunk enough.

Mr Gatt continued to down the liquor.

I have a very stressful job, he said finally. There are people demanding results. But what can we do? What can we offer them? We can't create something out of thin air, can we? We're not here to perform. We're here to keep an eye on what every-body else is up to. We can't help it if they're not up to anything.

He looked at me. Are they up to anything? He was giving me a last chance. I wanted to say what he wanted to hear, but all the evidence written down was to the contrary. Let me have a look at the transcripts, he said, as if he could read my mind. I fetched them and put them on the table in front of him.

He sat with his fingers in among the sheets of paper, having turned over the first page. What have they been up to, he muttered to himself, and better make it good. He looked up at me. Was he expecting me to answer him? I remained quiet and waited for the moment of expectation to pass. I saw the cloud of it leave his face and I knew I was off the hook. All he had to do was read the transcripts. He had a quick look, and I could see him forming an impression of me, from them, almost at once. It was a different impression of me than he'd had before. I had let him down. I wondered if he wasn't looking for a way out.

Your handwriting gives you away, he said.

What does my handwriting tell you?

You're in danger of not making yourself heard.

What do you mean?

He told me: Your writing is without personality.

Are you telling me it's too neat?

Not neat necessarily, he replied.

I told him my job left me no room for self-expression and that wasn't the reason he had hired me.

But nevertheless I could add a curl to my kicking k I think it used to be called when I was learning how to write it, or a flourish to the tails on the y or the q or the p. The p? Maybe not the p, he said, but certainly the f and g.

The devil is in the detail, he added, and I thought he might be right, after all there were all manner of things I knew nothing about that might be happening underneath a seemingly bland surface. I considered for a moment I could make it my job to unearth them. This also goes for his impression of me though, I thought.

Let yourself go, he said almost absent-mindedly.

We sat in silence while he pored some more over the documents. Occasionally he frowned at something.

There's nothing in here, he said finally.

No, I said.

What is all this? He tossed the transcripts aside. We sat, both of us eyeing the discarded document, before he turned and looked at me. I couldn't ignore his gaze for long.

If you want my advice on an altogether unrelated topic, he said, changing the subject, you're wise to stay out of management.

Yes, I said.

You're better off being in charge of nobody but yourself.

That's right, I thought. I requested another drink.

Where the fuck is she? He was suddenly talking about Mona again. You told her I was coming?

Yes, I said.

She knows anyway, she's been doing the job long enough. Listen, he said, pouring me another measure, I was hoping you would be a steadying influence on her. I'm a good judge of character. I could see you were a man who could see the job done. Am I right?

You are, I said.

But she's a contrary, back-to-front kind of bitch, he said. But of course you know that.

Actually I'm warming to her, I replied. He put his glass on the table so he could enjoy a chuckle. I came here to apologise, he said. I was ready to admit I had deceived you, in regard to Mona, and now this...

Although you're right she is contrary, I said instinctively because I didn't want him to misunderstand me: whatever had to be said about the moment of tenderness I had experienced with Mona, I knew it was first and foremost fragile. It existed, I was fully aware, in a fictional space that had been drawn up between Mona and myself, or rather by me, to contain it, and while I knew of its harmony with my world and that it surely touched hers somewhere, I was also aware Mr Gatt was too crude to understand it, especially when he was drunk.

Nevertheless he said let's drink to that, and we did, although he wasn't referring to her contrariness I realised, he was toasting my recognition of it, her contrariness I sensed he could do without.

So you're a little lovelorn, he said.

No, I replied. You're making incorrect assumptions.

He laughed at this too.

You miss the city, he said. You say you miss the city, but if Mona would show her face around here once in a while it'd be a different story.

I lowered my head.

And you've lost weight, he said.

I nodded.

I suppose that's for no one in particular? I looked at him. Even as we were talking the weight was falling off of me.

I've grown accustomed to not eating very much, I said, it's just turned out that way.

Mr Gatt tried to coerce me gently me into eating two pieces of the cake he had brought with him, just as he had coerced me into drinking the Armagnac, but I declined. I understood better now how he worked, he's what I would call a smooth operator. He begins by ingratiating himself into your confidence, maybe he inclines toward your camp in a slight disagreement; in any of the battles I have had with Mona, he's been on my side, and yet at the same time he always seems to give her the benefit of the doubt in some way. So I was wise to his manipulations. When the mild coercion, the threat he would be mortally offended if his hospitality was thrown back in his face, didn't work, he became more aggressive. He got up and tried to force the cake into my mouth. I fought him off and the cake became crumbs between his fingers. We jostled like this, some might think playfully, for a number of minutes and then Mr Gatt seemed to lose heart. He stopped a moment for a breather and it didn't take long for him to forget what he had in mind and eat the crumbs himself; many of the bits of cake never made it into his mouth and fell onto the tabletop or the floor. I put the whole episode down to the effects of the alcohol.

We drank a few more glasses.

I enjoyed some minutes of happiness, first of all because my borders hadn't been breached by the cake, and I was also heartened by the ever more obvious clarity of the realisation I had had earlier, namely that it was mainly my body feeling the ill-effects of the alcohol. My mind was free from any discomfort. It was released in fact from any of its previous inhibitions. While my body continued to ignore instructions there was something different in it now, it wasn't through rebellion it was because of a kind of paralysis. I was aware, as always, of my dislocation from my physical being but now I was happy to leave it unsupervised, without fear of what it might get up to. Of course I found comfort in this.

Mr Gatt began again to drum his fingers on the tabletop and it was both of us watching the fingers for a moment that caused them to suddenly lose the rhythm they had established and trip over themselves. Mr Gatt finally regained control of the hand by slapping the table with his palm. He picked up his glass and swallowed what was in it down in one.

In the long silence that followed we pursued a subject for conversation, and the noise that had been bothering Mona came up. Mr Gatt wondered what my views were on it.

I haven't heard any noise, I told him. He thought that kind of attitude was counter-productive.

What do you mean? I asked him. Can you hear it?

You may not think I have much time for Mona, he said, but you're very wide of the mark. This of course was not my view at all and I felt I ought to protest, but he began to speak again.

I take everything Mona brings to my attention very seriously, he said, after all isn't that the reason I employed her in the first place? I also have every faith in you, he went on to say, but I employed you for a different reason.

So what are you saying to me?

Where do you think the noise is coming from?

I was dumbstruck.

Do you think it's coming from outside?

No, I said.

So you think it's coming from inside the house?

Yes, I said, realising he had backed me into a corner.

Good man, he said in reply. We were both aware some progress had been made.

It was Mr Gatt's idea to take a look in the loft. He decided in his drunken state that whatever was making the noise must be up there. I made a half-hearted attempt to dissuade him and then I fetched a stepladder.

When I saw Mr Gatt up the ladder I realised that the hallway at the top of the stairs was the only room in the house that retained its original high ceiling, but I decided to keep the knowledge of this to myself in case he started knocking holes into the walls.

He ascended into the gloom; in fact he had already disappeared through the hole. I thought I'd never seen such blackness as was in that hole, nevertheless I followed him up. As I stuck my head through the ceiling Mr Gatt struck a match. The space he revealed was hemmed in by the limited throw of the light from the flame but it was clear enough that it was empty.

When the match went out I asked: What do you say to that?

I think we made too much noise, he answered, holding the next match up to his face. Whatever it is it's probably hiding in a corner somewhere.

I attempted to pull myself up into the loft space but I wasn't up to the task. The ladder occasionally shuddered under me.

I descended.

Mr Gatt didn't come down for some time. I stood on the landing waiting to see his legs appearing first, searching for a foothold on the ladder, and even though I began to think it a fruitless wait I didn't move, it was like waiting for a bus that never comes, still you never give up because the minute you abandon the wait the bus arrives. Eventually he appeared and I was still waiting. He seemed somewhat cowed by our adventure as if he had met some entity up in the loft, which had visited him after I had departed, and which had chastised him for his intrusion and more likely for his having revealed the hidden space to me. Whatever, his high spirits had certainly left him completely.

When he was standing again on the relative safety of the landing he took me to one side deliberately.

It was the drink that had made him forget himself he told me, it wasn't any of my business what was in the loft. He asked me if I remembered anything of what I had seen and I enquired as to what was supposed to be up there. He knocked me down the stairs to show me he meant business.

Mr Gatt slept in my bed. I lay for some time where I had landed and then I slept the rest of the night on the couch. He woke me up the next morning, early, and told me Mona had not been home.

You could have slept in her bed, he said.

I was feeling worse for wear because of the heavy drinking and the fact I'd been knocked close to unconsciousness and slept half the night at the foot of the stairs. Mr Gatt showed no signs of contrition for what he had done, nor did he regain any of his good humour.

After a cursory cup of coffee, which he drank standing outside in the yard, he came back into the kitchen. I was sitting at the table. He glared at me for a moment before Mona arrived. He must have seen her coming because she came in only a minute or two after him. It looked as if she hadn't seen him though, judging by the way she reacted when she saw us and all of our four eyes trained on her. Not surprisingly, I thought, she looked a little nonplussed, both her eyebrows were at half-mast.

Mona, said Mr Gatt. Mona didn't reply. Instead she handed me a tape.

I've been hearing all about your adventures, he said sarcastically, which caused Mona to turn her accusatory eye on me.

Don't fucking look at him like that, he said, you need to look at yourself.

Mona said nothing.

Look at your fucking self, he added in case she didn't get the message.

Mona looked at herself and then at her watch and that seemed to tire her out. She sat down at the table across from me. I thought, haven't we been here before, and she still had her coat on, which also rang a bell, but it was different this time of course because Mr Gatt was also with us, and his was an over-powering presence, made all the more so because of Mona's collapsed demeanour, which in better days might have diluted it. This must be a serious fault with her, I thought, because she would never have let her guard down and shown a vulnerable side of herself like this to Mr Gatt before. It was manifesting itself as a different kind of sadness to the sadness she exhibited the rest of the time, it was raw and close to the surface.

I wanted to say to her, I'm here for you, but I stopped myself just in time because as much as anything else it sounded sentimental, which I'm sure she wasn't a fan of. Instead I asked Mr Gatt to make himself clear. What have I been saying? I asked him because I didn't want Mona to think badly of me. It was negligible though whether she would have heard anything he'd said, she was looking down at her hands on the table, and at the fingers on her hands, which were picking at each other – not at the nails which were as bitten down as far as they could be, but at the bits of skin around the nails, so that in patches it was red raw and bleeding. In a minute she'll suck one of them to offer some kind of respite or release; it all adds to the impression of despair she's looking for.

Then she suddenly seemed to wake up.

I don't know what he's been saying, she said, talking about me, but he's not the person you should be talking to, not about any of this, and it was at this point she sucked her finger; I took the accompanying wince then to be a response to the finger she'd bitten to pieces, but I was also aware this was a presumption on my part, the wince might in fact be a symptom of her anger toward me, and the raw-looking flesh on the finger might have been made less raw with the few hours or days it'd been exposed to the air already, and as a result might not really be that painful, certainly not as painful as it looked. Anyhow when Mr Gatt said nothing she returned to furiously biting at the skin around her nails. It became all I could focus on such was the ferocity with which she attacked herself.

Leave them!

The fact I'd said this out loud surprised me. She stopped, I think because she was surprised too, and she placed her hands, palms upward, on the table. Then she looked me straight in the eye. I think I was expecting her eyes to be full of rage, but they weren't; in fact she looked lost somehow.

In the moment of silence that followed I said: I heard the noise that has been haunting you in the night, Mona.

She became slightly emotional when I confessed the noise had woken me. I said: I was covered in a cold sweat, and she almost cried to say that this was how it had happened the first time with her too.

I suggested by my tone that she and I had agreed as to its nature and whereabouts in a previous conversation, which of course we hadn't, although she now felt at liberty to state with some confidence that the noise had increased in volume since she had heard it first, and she wanted it noted that she was now more sure of herself than ever. In our previous discussion she was undermined by my negative reaction, but my admission, through my acknowledging of the noise and allowing it a life, had given it more credence in her eyes, an existence, I suppose, in her mind.

There it is again, I said. Mona's eyes lit up and I felt my heart warming.

What? Obviously Mr Gatt couldn't hear anything. Mona cast a sideways glance in his direction.

It's coming from the yard, she said. Mona had heard the noise before, of course.

There it is again, I said, and we went through the pantomime of listening, concentratedly, once more, Mr Gatt even more carefully, so that I thought he might strain himself, and Mona with the air of someone who had listened and had heard it and need not try to pick the sound out of an orchestra of other incidental noises again, who in fact is used to hearing it I suppose to the detriment of any other sound in the ether, so familiar had it become to her ear. This time she simply presumed it was there.

And again, I said, marking it this time with a downward stroke of my extended forefinger, as if I were making a further notch on the table edge.

You heard it, you heard it, Mona said gleefully.

By now it looked like Mr Gatt might explode. I was beginning to enjoy myself very much. Still Mr Gatt couldn't hear it, but there was now common ground between Mona and myself.

Mr Gatt must have decided at this point that there was actually something deficient in him, because he suddenly took a chance, by saying: Yes, there it is. It's a sort of banging, he added after a pause.

No, Mona said. I was able to concur with her.

It sounds like a banging to me, Mr Gatt reiterated.

A banging? I asked disbelievingly.

Well, more a sort of knocking, he said but now he was already more tentative.

No, said Mona, definitely not a knocking.

No from me again.

What then? he asked.

Not a banging, said I.

Not a knocking, said Mona.

What have I got left?

For pity's sake, Mona said.

He must have been wondering: a petting or a stroking perhaps, but how can you hear a stroking?

If you can't hear it you can't hear it, Mona said. He moaned,

I think like he imagined the noise might sound, and for a moment I thought he was going to strike me but he just wanted me to look into his ear.

I can hear it, he said, only the main body of the sound is dulled because of the wax in my ears. He tilted his head so I could take a look inside. The results of such a quick examination were inconclusive though. I told him I couldn't see why he couldn't hear. I'd need some sort of stick and a lamp to ascertain the problem.

We waited for him to calm down but he didn't. It was as if the absence of the noise was driving him mad. He thumped the side of his head with the palm of his hand to try and clear the blockage. He did this a number of times until his head had taken an almighty pummelling and was reeling from the self-inflicted blows. Suddenly he said: Can I have a word? and he got quickly to his feet and, walking in an arc or a spiral even, he went out of the back door; I'm not sure that was where he intended to end up.

For a second I sat and looked at Mona in the hope that it was her he wanted to talk to. She smiled. I got up and followed him out. When I'd closed the door behind me he immediately said: Listen, you prick, I don't know what you're playing at but you're singing from a different hymn sheet all of a sudden and I want to know why.

I pretended I was distracted again by the sound just as I was about to reply to him. We both looked into the bushes around and about.

I'm going, he said suddenly.

What? I asked.

You obviously can't keep the necessary eye on yourself, he said, but you can watch her. When she asks what I wanted to talk to you about tell her I gave you a dressing-down.

Why? I asked.

She thinks everyone is against her, this will only add fuel to the fire. The first thing she'll think is we're out here plotting against her. I turned to look in the window. I needn't have worried because Mona was still sitting at the table with her back to us.

She's a fucking contrary bitch, he went on to say, and that's what I'm worried about. I ought to have pegged you back there and then, in front of her, but suddenly I couldn't bear the hypocrisy of it all. Anyhow, as you can see, he said, I've put myself in a rather compromising position.

I told him I didn't know what he was talking about.

I mean, he said deliberately, that I've rushed out here without my bag.

So what do you want me to do?

I had to go back into the house for his case. I went around the house and put all the things he had left lying around into it: his glasses, his cigarettes, his wallet, a few coins, his retractable pencil, the file of papers I had transcribed for him, yesterday's newspaper, and then I went to the bathroom to fetch his toothbrush, his toothpaste, his shampoo and body wash in a bottle, his razor and shaving foam, his after-shave, his comb, his deodorant and his watch, which he had left on the side of the bath.

When I returned to the kitchen some time later, because it took me some time, I found Mona standing at the sink looking out of the window at Mr Gatt, who was doing his best to appear invisible. She didn't look at me at all as I went out with the bag. I passed it to Mr Gatt, who snatched it out of my hand. He opened it and took stock of the contents, making sure I suppose that I'd collected everything. As he turned to leave he told me what else he suddenly had on his mind: My visits are prescribed to put your minds at rest, he said, but at the same time I can only work with what you've given me. The lack of any discernable plot in the papers you have given me does not constitute failure as such.

It's our job to write the news, I said as if by rote, not to make it.

That might be right, he replied, but I must remind you no news is bad news. Can you pass that sentiment on to Mona?

I sensed his frustration and I was overcome with a feeling of hopelessness. Was he expecting something from me? And if so, what? The silence that followed began to bait me and, while I had no idea how he might be bearing up under its demands, I knew I couldn't bear it any longer, so impulsively I said: She's on to something very big, which was followed by another silence, a much shorter one admittedly, it might only have been a moment's hesitation on his part actually.

What a star, he said through gritted teeth. Now you tell her from me to get her fucking act in order.

When he had gone I turned round and looked at Mona's face which was framed in the window, it was giving nothing away, she looked vacantly out, but by the time I got back into the kitchen she was looking at me expectantly.

He's gone, I said.

What did he want? Mona asked.

He had a go at me, I said, for speaking to you like that.

What?

It's not my place.

Like what? She spoke incredulously. It was at this moment I felt some sort of alliance had been forged between us despite everything that had happened; it took me a little by surprise, but I liked it nevertheless.

What the hell is he on? she asked.

Don't you worry about Mr Gatt, I said to her.

When she discovered a couple of days later that I had invented the noise for the benefit of Mr Gatt she stormed out and although I didn't know it at the time I would never see her again.

the development

Jack is the first to give voice to his feelings about the venue he has selected for their second meeting with Mr Scrivener. He is delighted.

Do you know why I love the park, he asks exuberantly, but he isn't going to get a reply from Jill, and he knows it, so decides to answer the question himself: *because I love the smell of new-mown grass.*

Of course when he puts it like that I can almost smell it myself, but it's the worst kind of thing to say to Jill, who suffers from hay fever. She decides there and then that in future she'll make decisions like this herself, I mean about where meetings will be held. In fact a lot of things are going to be done differently. All of her dissatisfaction is plain to see. She isn't a woman who hides her feelings very well and if Jack had any kind of sensitivity he might have picked up on her discontent for himself.

I imagine them sitting side by side on one of the benches usually reserved for parents watching their children play on the swings.

Jack can probably feel Jill's anger, and this is something he'll likely address in a minute or two, but for the moment he is carefree, maybe he's imagining he's having a go on the swings himself; he thinks about the rush of air, at first in his face and then against the back of his head, and for the split second when he's at the top of the swing, neither moving forwards nor swinging back, everything becomes clear to him. The rest of the time, he thinks, I am fighting against the tide, thinking about going somewhere, and when finally I am on my way, thinking about what I will find when I get there, only to wonder what I shall do when I leave, when I have arrived.

Time in the park passes by more slowly perhaps than anywhere else. Jill must be looking at her watch because Jack asks her what time it is.

Why don't you wear a watch?

Jack doesn't respond.

He's late anyway, Jill reports.

A few more minutes pass before Jack speaks again. *I used to come to this park as a boy,* he says.

Is that why you chose it for the meeting?

I thought it might be more private.

Look around you.

I know.

We're surrounded by kids and their parents and by heaven knows who else, and suddenly her words conjure them up for me, the kids, out of nothing; I can hear them now, shouting and crying, their mothers and fathers talking to each other. I can even hear the sound of the odd dog barking in the distance. I hear everything more clearly now as if their acknowledging it has given it life.

Jill wipes her nose again. The pollen is reaching all the way up to her sinuses. I can hear her sniffing. Did Jack know about this when he arranged the rendezvous, I wonder. Maybe he did it in order to undermine her authority.

I imagine Jack picking up the phone. He is standing in his grey office and he happens to glance out of the window. Suddenly there are leaves on all the trees, he hadn't noticed, and he has the desire to stretch his legs outside, so when Mr Scrivener picks up the phone at the other end Jack suggests the park as a place to meet. His voice travels all the way down the wire to Mr Scrivener, who doesn't know of any park, at least not in the vicinity Jack is describing. Of course there's a lovely little park, Jack used to play there as a boy. Oh there, says Mr Scrivener, not in response to Jack having played there as a boy of course, but due to some reconsideration on his part and perhaps to the further instructions Jack is giving him. Isn't there anywhere else a bit closer in, Mr Scrivener thinks, but too late or too slowly, because Jack has already put the phone down on him. All that is left is for Mr Scrivener to think: that bastard has called me and caught me on the hop, suggesting a place as if it's already been agreed, and before I can get my bearings, he's hung up. Here I am at this end, still holding the receiver, deciding to make sure Jack never gets the better of me like this again.

He puts the handset down and lights a cigarette, which he kids himself calms his nerves, when in truth it does exactly the opposite. He picks up the phone again to confirm his course of action with a third party and is told, that's right, nothing has changed.

Later when they are in the park Jill is wishing she could dispense with Jack's services once and for all, while at the same time she's aware that anybody who works for the Council is in the job for life. She wants to say to him, don't think you're safe, although of course he is, so instead she asks him: *Where is he then?*

Here he comes, says Jack and immediately he arrives and I can tell he isn't in the best of moods, it's as if the air crackles with static as soon as he appears. To make matters worse I realise there probably isn't any room for him on the bench either, not that he'd want to sit next to either Jack or Jill anyhow because then a line would be formed and any subsequent words of dialogue would have to be spoken loudly, probably too loudly if it contained secret information, or else passed down the line by the body sitting in the middle, and the body in the middle would surely do damage to its neck as it sat swivelling the head back and forth between the converser on one side of it and the listener on the other, and when it was the body in the middle's turn to do the talking, which way would it turn to direct its invective, to the left first or to the right?

In any event Mr Scrivener decides to stay on his feet and look down on Jack; from up here he can feel as if he is the one in charge, and for a moment Jack contemplates standing himself, at first it's the natural thing to do if he's going to greet Mr Scrivener, but Mr Scrivener straight away starts talking business to them, with no attention afforded to any kind of pleasantries, and so removing from Jack his god-given rights.

He kicks off with a statement. *My contact tells me there's nothing in it*, he says.

Jack is still taken aback. *Excuse me*, he says and maybe he contemplates getting to his feet again here as well, to be in a better position to defend himself if he should need to, but he worries everything has run out of his control when he discovers Mr Scrivener is standing so close that their shins are almost touching, as well as their knees (before Jack's thighs go off horizontally and at 90 degrees). The upshot of this is that Jack can't gain the leverage he needs to get up. Naturally you see, he would slide forward slightly to get his feet under him, after all it's the feet which have to hold the whole thing up, but Mr Scrivener, by his positioning, isn't allowing him the space to complete the manoeuvre. Jack turns momentarily, in a panic, toward Jill, to see if she can come to his rescue, but she is seemingly unperturbed. Maybe she isn't seeing it as he is.

Can you be more specific? she asks Mr Scrivener calmly.

They're having a patio laid in their back garden, Mr Scrivener replies.

What? says Jack. *What did you say?* He turns to Jill. *What did he say?*

What's the matter with you? asks Jill.

I don't like this, Jack replies.

You don't have to like it, says Jill, and then after a pause she addresses Mr Scrivener again: *How reliable is your contact?* she asks.

Reliable enough, he replies.

And I don't think the Leader of the Town Council even knows that much about it. It looks to me like it might have been his wife doing all the negotiating.

This is the man she's been seen speaking to?

Yes, says Mr Scrivener. *But more to the point,* he adds, *this man in the Building Control Department has been on sick leave, and has recently been awarded an indefinite period of absence.*

What with?

A bad back.

Then he's not fit to be laying patios, says Jill.

He's not fit to be laying anything, says Mr Scrivener.

And that's all you've got? asks Jack.

Mr Scrivener turns to Jill as if he'd like her to put Jack on a leash.

What else? asks Jill.

Your man in the Building Control Department hasn't been telling you the whole story.

Mr Ledger?

Yes.

I can't believe what I'm hearing, says Jack.

Go on, says Jill.

There's a second man in the Building Control Department who's in on it.

And a further exasperated inhalation from Jack.

In on what?

In on the patio-laying job, replies Mr Scrivener.

What's his involvement?

He's going to be driving the van, says Mr Scrivener.

What van?

They take paving slabs from an existing council job, in a council van, at the weekend, and the second man drives the van.

And Mr Ledger is covering for him?

I don't know whether he's covering for him or he just hasn't seen fit to mention him.

Why would he cover for him?

I don't know.

So what about all our work, Jack enquires of Jill. *Are we going to take this man seriously?*

Be quiet, says Jill.

Listen, says Mr Scrivener, *I didn't look into it any further because I don't feel it's worth wasting any more time over. I didn't get involved in order to uncover a small-time building scam. From what you were telling me I was expecting some sort of grand monetary windfall. This is about some petty pilfering of building materials and the illegal use of a council van.*

If any of them had looked up at that moment and cast their gazes to the far side of the recreation field, across the cricket square in summer cum football pitch in winter, they would have seen me entering the park. Look, I'm striding toward them with some purpose.

As I walk the hundred metres or so, potentially always in sight of them, I consider how I'd like them to perceive me, but the more aware I am that their eyes might be on me, the more awkwardly I feel I am walking; every step in the end becomes torturous. It's as if I have forgotten how to walk. I tell myself: lift the left leg, you arsehole, like this, and put it down again in front, you can presume the rest, that the ground is going to be there, for example, and remember to look natural – now the right, and so on.

Actually before I go any further let me tell you how I have come to be here. I am holding on to the notion that I can get a closer look at events. From the outside listening in I can see the whole thing coming apart at the seams, I am watching it funnel itself into a dead end, and that's going to be the finish of the story, that's what I think, and we're not even half the way through it, so here I am, trying to make a difference. I think if I can find an opportunity to speak to Jack and Jill I might be able to rescue this fiasco from the ignoble fate it seems destined to suffer.

But it isn't as easy as all that, I discover almost straight away, because the rot has already set in. While I have been walking and they have been talking, my positive outlook has already begun to darken; the clouds have come over. For a start I am thinking about all my imperfections, which might seem superfluous to the picture I am painting of the wider world outside, but are in fact integral to the way I am painting it. I don't just mean that I suddenly can't remember how to walk properly, although it was probably this realisation that set me off on this negative train of thought in the first place, but I realise I don't really have an imagination that's up to the task. Come to think of it, as I stand in this landscape barren of any kind of detail, any sumptuous colour or arty monochrome, I realise that my mind's eye is actually myopic: all the places I picture when I am expected to picture a place are done out in the same way: if it's indoors it's always with the same cheap carpet, never patterned, and off-white walls; occasionally I might spot a bit of pine furniture. And the same goes for any place I imagine outdoors, more so in fact: take this park I imagine myself in now, for example, it's certainly nothing to get excited about. The grass is uniform green as you might expect, like in a children's colouring book, there are no patches of mud or areas of moss, although as I mention them now perhaps they begin to spring up, I don't know. I can't even imagine the lines of the football pitch because I have forgotten how they are marked out, I know there's an eighteen-yard box, but what is it eighteen yards from, and a centre circle that threatens to collapse the park in on itself, like a black hole, and the goalposts frame nothing but a patch of blue-grey sky. That's just bloody wonderful. And the edges of the park are vaguer still; if I attempt to focus on what lies on the borders, my attention is immediately taken up with something else, anything else, I don't know what, what is there?

Then in the flurry of all these thoughts I realise my legs have suddenly, and without recourse to any kind of democratic ballot held with any of the other parts of my body, stopped walking. I have come to a standstill, my left leg still cocked out though, in front of me. I bring it back to earth with some force and press on.

When I next look up I see in front of me the same play-ground arrangement – a roundabout, swings and a slide – that I recall from my childhood, you see what I mean about the lack of imagination? And if I picture a child any child on any of the apparatus of course it is myself, unidentifiable maybe from here, except for the striped jumper I am wearing which I remember, and this is regardless of the fact I cannot be in this place, which in truth is not the place Jack and Jill, nor Mr Scrivener are in, at either one of these two times. I feel I have added myself at the last minute because somebody has to make use of the swings. Surely I can ascertain from this that all the other children and their mothers have disappeared, or is it that I never really imagined them as anything other than voices in the first place? So what, I neglected to people the park with anyone except for Jack and Jill, who sit on the bench, and standing up in front of them, that must be Mr Scrivener, the man from the Strategic Planning and Investment Team. They all look exactly as I pictured them, but you might have expected that. I realise I have failed to add Mona to the gathering. An oversight. Also I can't formulate a picture in my head of what is happening beyond the bench they are sitting on, I admit it. The world might be flat and they might be on the very edge of it, hanging over the drop; the blue sky falls down behind them like a theatrical curtain.

As I stride the last few steps up to them, still purposefully I might add – the left leg thrown out and then moments later the right pulled up to join it – Mr Scrivener or better still Jack (Mr Scrivener still has his back to me after all), might become aware of my approach. If he's talking he might stop, and his silence might alert Mr Scrivener, while Jill I imagine has spotted me already, she might smile inwardly or in a small outwardly way and believe I have come to resuscitate her from this dull existence, and indeed I have, and Mr Scrivener might turn at this point, his thin moustache twitching madly on his top lip, after all this is an unexpected turn of events, has he been double-crossed, he has every right to wonder, in fact he might very well ask, who the hell is this?

But I walk beyond the three of them straight away and do not even pass the time of day. I sit on the swings next to the boy in the striped jumper. He has already allowed the momentum of the swing that was carrying him upwards over the park to come to a standstill and as he hangs there he looks at me with something of a puzzled expression on his face. For a second I think I might kill him to spare him all of his subsequent travails, but before I can raise my hand against him I am alerted to the fact Mr Scrivener is leaving the park. I don't watch him go, it's enough I know it for it to come to pass. Instead I walk over to Jack and Jill, who are still sitting on the bench. It only takes a moment before they acknowledge me. Jack, I think, expects another similar assault as he has already suffered this afternoon at the hands of Mr Scrivener, but Jill simply asks me: *Who are you?*

Of course I have already made sure Mona has commented in my transcription thus: *The second person has revealed himself.*

I am the driver, I hear myself say, and Jack and Jill were reported to have heard me say it, Mona was reported to have recorded it and I to have subsequently transcribed it. In truth it doesn't matter what might have been said or heard or recorded, it only matters what I transcribe. I was suddenly giddy with the realisation of the power I held.

Anyhow I would imagine the driver's admission causes a

small charge, like electricity, to pass between Jack and Jill; she might be able to hide it, but Jack grins a little like a child because he cannot stop himself.

How did you find us? Jill wants to know.

I followed Mr Scrivener. You see how I'm thinking on my feet?

Jack is at least given the satisfaction of imagining Mr Scrivener leading him to them through his incompetence; he's not taking into account any of the likely consequences of course, nor the notion that maybe Mr Scrivener did it on purpose.

Nevertheless you've gone out of your way, Jill says.

It was only a slight diversion actually, and in all honesty the driver, as I imagine him, does not believe any place is out of his way, not when he is driving. I look at the driver's watch. *I can't stay long,* he says, *I still have some miles to put on the clock.*

I stopped writing for a moment to consider what I had done. Any reservations I might suddenly be having had to be short-lived because, as the character of the driver, I was as real now, in the world I was transcribing, as Jack and Jill.

It was obvious to me, as I was listening to that last conversation between Jack and Jill and Mr Scrivener, that Mr Gatt would not be satisfied with the way things were panning out. I envisaged, as a consequence of this, the conclusion of the job, and to avoid the subsequent break-up of Mona and myself as a team, which I didn't want – and I was surprised at myself for thinking this – I decided to craft an ending of my own making.

First I stopped the tape. I had a moment or two wondering what else might be on it, a moment to reappraise the situation, it being the last chance I had to turn back from the course of action I had decided upon. I was inflamed though with the thought of all the possibilities open to me and I was in thrall to the character of the driver, who was already forming so clearly in my mind. I had taken the tape out of the machine and had it in my hand when I imagined Jack and Jill procrastinating about which pastry to have, whether to sit at this café table or that one, and I allowed their voices to drift away from me as if in a dream. I felt no guilt either, after all wouldn't I be giving them a new lease of life, a life they could never envisage, and if they could a life they would hanker after? I watched Jack on his way home, another day having passed him by in his pursuit of a better life, and I was reminded of myself, sitting in my old flat, overlooking the dead landscape.

I hankered after this new life too; in fact I became euphoric when I imagined what might be in store for me.

I put the tape back into the machine and rewound it as I did with all the tapes I had finished with. Then I took it out and placed it in the pile with all the others. I spent most of the next day recording over all the used tapes I had accrued since I had been here so that there was only static left on them.

That was when it was decided and couldn't be reversed. I would somehow augment Mona's reports with additions of my own that were more interesting and that would go some way to satisfying Mr Gatt's brief. Of course, with hindsight, it's easy to see that only disaster can come of a strategy like this, but at the time I was convinced that, whatever I decided to write, it didn't matter, it would prove to be a manageable situation. Mona didn't have to know anything about it either, I figured she was never around when Mr Gatt called and it didn't seem to me an impossible task to keep them apart.

I thought about the driver some more before I committed him to paper. I asked myself, at the onset, given an opportunity like this, is it better to persevere with the personality you've been given, or consider making some improvements? I spent some time pondering on all my faults and thought that I had the chance to put some of them right in the make-up of the driver; although I knew I would only be the basic template for the resulting man, he would also take on a life of his own. In truth, so easily was the character of the driver flowing out of me unchecked, I wanted to take a moment to reflect. He is almost a solid man in front of me already, I thought, in front of my mind's eye, which I suppose is to be expected considering he resembles me physically in every way, just as you might imagine he would when you have a man like me, with a lazy mind's eye like I have, making him up.

When I imagine him walking about the place I am out of body, I look down on affairs and describe what I see. He is a healthy-enough-looking specimen, if a little on the heavy side. Fortunately I could put his excess bulk down to a life behind the wheel; when would he get the chance to think about exercising?

Over and above that he is charged with driving in all his working hours, I told myself, which he is more than happy to do, because he is happiest when he is behind the wheel. But it hasn't always been like this. As a small boy in short trousers he used to dream of a life on the road, but it remained only a dream and he lived a sedentary life because of it; all his natural desires were thwarted by his lack of wheels. So when the calling finally came it didn't come from where he expected it to either. After all how could that small boy have imagined a job driving for the council? The life of derring-do he had invented in its stead though was perhaps only half a lie.

The day he was trusted with the keys he got into the van and he drove and drove and he didn't look back until one day he had to stop at the red traffic lights, and as soon as he stopped the ecstatic condition he had been enjoying was destroyed; he shut his eyes and submitted, maybe only momentarily, but long enough to be vulnerable, to the stationary state, which was where he was when he was visited by a man who leant in through the open side window.

Your man in the Building Control Department paid me a visit, the driver says to Jack and Jill.

Do you mean Mr Ledger? asks Jill.

He wanted to offer me a job.

I imagine the driver allows Jack the room to stand, should he want to, because he doesn't want to offer himself as a threat. Maybe Jack immediately feels there is no danger and chooses not to stand.

Is this about the Leader of the Town Council's patio? asks Jill.

I told him I already have a job driving for the council but your Mr Ledger is not the kind of man who will take no for answer.

Actually it was never about arm-twisting. It went more like this: Whatever his duties might be, the one constant is that the driver is nearly always driving, and it's during those moments when he's off-duty that he wants to be behind the wheel, and now here was a man suddenly offering him out-of-hours driving work. Maybe the ecstatic condition might come over him again, he thinks, beginning perhaps as a tingling sensation in his hand clutching the gear stick, and radiating outwards, into his accelerator pedal foot and beyond.

Can I unburden myself? the driver says.

Go ahead.

I'm happy to do the driving, he says, *but I'm not happy to have to come here to try and recruit you.*

I see, says Jill.

Do you? asks Jack.

I've been sent here by Mr Ledger to recruit you.

Recruit us to what? asks Jill.

We already have jobs, says Jack. *We work for the council.*

Jack is thinking all the time that he knows a very different Mr Ledger. He thinks he is on very good terms with the Mr Ledger he knows and is confused by this recent turn of events. The Mr Ledger he knows picks up the phone and speaks to him directly. Why would he involve a third person as a go-between? Jack is a very noisy thinker, there is always a garbled soundtrack to accompany his ruminations. Jill, of course, is familiar with it and is not sidetracked. *What kind of work is he offering us?* she enquires.

Surveillance work, says the driver.

He wants us to watch somebody? Jill suddenly comes to life. She has suffered weeks of dead ends and disappointments, all her expectations for the mission have time and again led to nothing, but now there is a sparkle in her eye.

We surveil already for the council, says Jack.

Is it after-hours surveillance work? Jill wants to know.

I only know it's surveillance work.

If it's surveillance work, says Jill, *that's a different matter altogether.*

We're the best surveillance team in the business, says Jack, as if it's a line he's been rehearsing.

Who does he want surveilling? asks Jill.

Mr Ledger is working on a development project and he wants one of his partners tailed.

Does he have a name?

He works in the Building Control Department.

Of course Jack and Jill already have their eye on a man who works in the Building Control Department and Jack is already thinking of ways they could do the two jobs at the same time and make twice the money.

What's his name?

Mr Wood.

Leave him to us, says Jill, a smile on her face.

I took my notepad out into the yard and sat on one of the chairs that had seen better days, located to the front of the house on what had laughingly been described by Mr Gatt, during his tour, as a terrace.

I was liberated of my headphones, and could wander where I pleased. I suspect, like the breakdown of my physical restraints, my imagination was also free to go to places it had never conceived of while it had been held under confinement in the study.

The sun was out and as the day progressed the patio turned into a sun terrace and then a suntrap.

I looked over what I had written so far.

Minutes after the driver has left the park and is back behind the wheel were he belongs Jack and Jill make a start. They return to the Town Hall, where the Building Control Depart-ment has an office. When they get there and make enquiries of a Mr Wood they discover he has taken sick leave and isn't expected to be back at work in the near future. What do we do now? Jack asks. Jill is sure it can't be difficult to find out where

Mr Wood lives. And so it proves. Following a visit to the personnel department they are on their way round to Mr Wood's house.

Jill tells Jack to drive once around the block to be certain they haven't been followed and they park up outside Mr Wood's house; it isn't difficult to find a place to park with a clear view of the front porch, although the car is somewhat conspicuous because all the residents park their cars in their garages.

They haven't been sitting there for long when a van pulls up outside. Mr Wood leaves his house and climbs into the back of it. Mr Ledger introduces him as Mr W and the driver acknowledges him in his rear-view mirror. As he pulls away the driver sees Jack and Jill parked a short distance down the street and he almost waves.

Before they're half a mile down the road Mr Wood points out they're being followed. The driver turns to Mr Ledger, who looks out of the back window.

You're sure?

Yes.

Lose them, Mr Ledger says to the driver and the driver loses them.

They pick up Mr Scrivener next. Hi, he says as he settles down beside Mr Wood in the back of the van. The last person they pick up is the Leader of the Town Council.

While they wait for him in his sitting room, the Leader of the

Town Council's wife serves them with shortbread biscuits on a plate. The driver partakes with Mr Scrivener and Mr Wood while Mr Ledger abstains. You have a very nice home, he says, to pass the time of day while they wait, not really because he means it, although he looks at the horse brasses as if he's a fan. There is also a collection of pillboxes in a display cabinet. He bends forward so he can better examine them through the glass window. The driver remains in a more defensive upright stance, while none of them take up the deferential attitude, on their knees, although all of them are well aware of the lofty position held by the Leader of the Town Council, and by association his wife. Mr Ledger obviously feels impelled to make some reference to this obliquely with the comment: I'm in the Minor Works Project Design and Management Services.

Ah, says the Leader of the Town Council's wife, nodding, although his qualifications probably mean very little to her, living as she does out here on the very periphery of council business.

Mr Wood here works for the Building Control Department, Mr Ledger continues, gesturing, and she nods again, with a small knowing smile to accompany it. Mr Scrivener is with the Strategic Planning and Investment Team, says Mr Ledger, and this, he concludes, is the driver. The Leader of the Town Council's wife turns to look at him.

I love to drive, is all the driver can say.

There's a television on in the corner of the room. Suddenly,

in the uncomfortable silence, it takes on a magnified importance, momentarily the gathering look, as one, at the flickering
screen. A man is shouting at his cheating wife. Soon he storms
out and the wife turns to the decanter of whisky on the
sideboard. The camera moves in for a close-up of her face. She
grimaces as the spirit takes her breath away, unaccustomed as
she is to it; it allows her to express her anguish as if by proxy
though.

The Leader of the Town Council's wife has half an eye on the
proceedings, this being her favourite soap; she often used to sit
alone, living her emotionally dead life vicariously through the
adventures of the feuding families populating the storylines;
now though she has her affair with Mr Wood to make her life
worth living, and she no longer sees the woman as the villain
she used to, how can she be blamed for falling in love with
someone else, she says to herself.

She is still holding the plate of biscuits in her hand. The
feeding men gather around her in a loose semi-circle. Mr Wood
is unsure which biscuit he likes the look of and he spends a
moment longer with his hand hovering over the selection. The
Leader of the Town Council's wife mistakes his procrastinating
for flirting and smiles, which he notices (he decides to accept
her misunderstanding and use it perhaps to his advantage
later).

Just then the Leader of the Town Council walks into the
room. He is a squat little man with a brusque manner. He is

buttoning his waistcoat as he moves among the men.

You have a lovely home, Mr Ledger repeats for his benefit and the Leader of the Town Council looks around for the briefest second as if he is surprised by the revelation, as if he has never spent any time considering the house he lives in, and indeed he hasn't, and looking at it now he is surprised by some of the choices his wife has made in furnishing it. Maybe he doesn't know her as well as he thought he did. The Leader of the Town Council is almost unaware of any of these thoughts going through his head though, so quickly does he brush them aside in order that he can quickly get on with the business at hand.

We'd better be going, he says.

When will you be home? his wife asks him.

I won't be long, he replies.

On the television the woman is on the phone, but she mumbles; the Leader of the Town Council's wife struggles to hear what she is plotting as the men thank her for the biscuits and make their way into the hall. Mr Wood is the last to leave the room and when he reaches the door he turns back and winks.

Of course I'll make sure I'm not followed, the woman on the television says and she hangs up the phone. The adulteress is climbing into her car as the men leave the house, and looking both ways they see the street is empty except for a man mowing his front lawn; he stops and watches as the group of men reconvene to the van, but if he is asked later he won't be able to name or describe any of them except his neighbour, the Leader of the Town Council, who is already making himself comfortable in the front seat.

When they're back on the road the Leader of the Town Council stresses the expedition is to be treated as strictly off-the-record and consequently not open to discussion outside of this circle of immediate interested parties. Everyone agrees to this without exception; although the driver says nothing, his assent is presumed from his silence.

They plunge head-first into the greenbelt itself. The tracks they end up driving down are barely roadworthy, and get less and less so as they advance deeper into the foliage, which in turn becomes thicker and denser.

The van is finally parked on the edge of what we discover is the site of a property development. The plan is to build an estate of luxury one-bedroom flats on greenbelt land.

Each of the men get out of the van in their own fashion. The air is thick with the noise of crickets and birds and other jungle creatures and damp with the overnight shower.

Preparation of the site itself has already begun. The area is cordoned off with yellow and black police tape and within it the grasses are laid flat and the small hills are brought under control and the earth they contained has been used to fill in all the divots and small valleys so that the field is without inclines up or down. All the native flora and fauna have been driven out into the surrounding high grass until not a single living thing lives therein.

The five men walk onto the site.

As the tape is lifted to allow them access and they cross the threshold all sounds and all sensations on the skin are suddenly erased as if they are entering into a vacuum, and they stand dumbstruck, Mr Wood with the cordon still raised high in his right hand. The Leader of the Town Council meanwhile seems relatively unfazed as he strides forth into the centre of the field and throws wide his arms, and there he communicates with himself, or with his god, out of earshot of everyone else. Mr Ledger turns to look at the rest of the party. It's his baby, he says as if in explanation.

Is anybody else having the same strange sensation as myself? asks Mr Scrivener working the end of his finger into his left ear.

This is what it must have been like when they landed on the moon, says Mr Wood.

That's a fine analogy, says Mr Scrivener in reply.

Mr Wood has released the tape and is bending down to the ground. He allows the earth to run through his fingers. It's fine, like sand, he says.

What did you expect? asks Mr Ledger.

The Leader of the Town Council meanwhile has turned back to face the men, his arms still in the air. Come on, boys, he calls and his voice carries across the empty distance to reach each and every one of them simultaneously. They all tentatively follow where the Leader of the Town Council has led, across the stripped earth.

Upon further inspection it is apparent that each holding within the area is marked out individually and it's clear where the base of each apartment block will stand. Imagine the buildings growing up out of the grasses to finally reveal to the outside world the work that has been taking place there, only far too late for the outside world to have any hope of stopping it.

In deference to the potential luxury one-bedroom flats the men intuitively stick to what will be the paved areas between the blocks, and here and everywhere else on the site, the earth, perhaps made aware of its imminent suffocation, makes the most of its last breaths of fresh air.

If we build them high enough, the Leader of the Town Council is saying as the group come to stand beside him, they'll all have a view of the sea.

There follows a tour of the site, during which Mr Wood goes to various points, at each corner and a number of other spots, and picks up soil, which he then allows to run through his fingers. The Leader of the Town Council makes himself available for questions. Mr Ledger asks something about which facilities included in the project will be made available to the community at large and Mr Scrivener is hoping to receive recommendations that matching funding is going to be made available from public coffers to add to that he has already secured from local business partnerships. All of it goes over the head of the driver; he just wants to get back on the road.

Mr Ledger meanwhile takes him to one side and tells him he is more than satisfied with his conduct so far, reminding him he had known all along who was the right man for the job. He tells the driver to expect a visit from him at any moment with further instructions. The thought Mr Ledger might suddenly appear again, as was his wont, fills the driver with terror. Consequently all the traffic lights they come across on their way back into town seem to be working against him.

The driver parks up in the council car park and in the foyer of the Town Hall is directed by the security guard on the front desk to take the lift to the third floor and when he steps out of the lift is told to take the first turning on the left and then the first right and so on until he will be completely lost. He looks up in the hope that something will be able to guide him back out, but the ceiling is a grid of strip lights, every one exactly the same. In this strange world lit by fluorescent light, he longs for the comfort of his cab.

Although the office is supposed to be open-plan it is in fact a series of enclosures marked out by partitions, a maze of corridors and work-stations; every council officer to their own enclosure, and every one obscured by the partitions that construct it; they stand just a few inches taller than the driver so he is unable to get his bearings.

He stands still for a moment and listens out for the sound of voices. He hears a man's voice and heads towards it, and in this way, more by accident than design, he ends up where he is supposed to be. On arrival he finds Jack sitting on Jill's knee. Jack appears to be more angry than embarrassed at being discovered; he takes his thumb out of his mouth and goes off to fetch two more chairs so everybody can sit comfortably. Meanwhile the driver looks around, familiarising himself with Jill's personal work-station: of course there is a desk with the requisite computer on it; there's a cuddly toy, an animal of some description, wedged under the monitor, as good as forgotten; a single swivel chair; post-it notes posted variously, and on each a hastily scrawled message to herself: shopping list; the first motion of the day; the second motion; a further predicted movement from here to there perhaps, and so on; a list of dates. There's also a pile of recycled scrap paper, an in-tray full of thin brown folders, a memo written in response to a memo received, and to one side a memo ignored, a pot of pencils, a pot of pens (perhaps they could all be put in the one pot), a stapler, a hole punch, photographs of her family and friends tacked on the wall, a motivational phrase taped in some predominant position, a wall calendar marked with meetings and birthdays and days taken off and days to be taken off, projecting her life forwards at least until the end of the year.

When his eyes finally settle on Jill he sees that she is already examining him, with such scrutiny he has to look away; he attempts to justify this by examining again the cuddly toy as if he's interested to know what species of animal it actually is.

Jack returns with two plastic chairs only for Jill to place her forefinger on her lips and silently direct them outside, after all the walls have ears, she tells them when they're in the car park, and the partitions wouldn't even qualify as walls, which meant they were asking for trouble.

Of course when they're in the car park the driver becomes distracted immediately by the van he has parked nearby. He suggests they all adjourn to the front seat, which he compliments because of its unusually roomy dimensions, but Jack suspects a trap and suggests the memorial garden nearby. Jill decides they will retreat to their usual café. Now I can see it for myself, I think.

There are seats outside and they take them, because here too, in the town, the sun is out, it beats down on them unrelentingly. The café is on the corner of the street that enters the square from the south. Impulsively I decide it looks onto Jack's memorial garden. That's the lazy third eye again I suppose and the realisation of this obviously irritates me because I wilfully notice it isn't the waitress I've always imagined who serves us, this is one I have to make up from scratch. She is a woman in her late twenties and she isn't wearing a wedding ring. She also treats Jack as if she has never met him before. We order coffees and nothing is said until they arrive. When they do Jack allows three packets of sugar to run slowly into his. The driver watches him do this as if hypnotised, as do I, and so does Mona, who is sitting a table or two away. Only Jill has seen it enough times to look away.

Finally the driver breaks the spell. *What have you got for me?* he asks.

Is that supposed to be a joke? Jack asks.

No.

We lost you, says Jill.

What the fuck were you doing? Jack is clearly angry.

Mr Wood noticed you were following us, the driver replies. *What choice did I have?*

You deliberately lost us though? says Jack.

The driver becomes momentarily morose. He swills the dregs of his coffee around in his cup as if he is reading the grounds before he pulls his chair forward; now he's sitting closer to the table and he rests what are my forearms on the surface in front of him and tells Jack and Jill about the visit to the site of the development.

How do we know we can trust you? Jack asks as soon as the driver has finished telling his story.

I can't do anything to help you with that, the driver says. *Trust me or don't.*

Jack moodily spoons the sugar crystals out of the bottom of his empty cup into his mouth.

Jill has already turned involuntarily to look west from their table and she imagines the apartments rising up between them and the coastline. Jack watches her as she shields her eyes against the sun.

The weather remained fine in the following week, it seemed the sun was rarely behind a cloud during the daylight hours. When Mr Gatt arrived for his second visit he took me by surprise. I didn't hear his car until I saw it pulling up down the side of the house. I went out to meet him. He immediately retired to the terrace without setting a foot inside. He took his shoes off and placed them side-by-side under his seat; I saw a toe poking through one of his socks, as if he had allowed it a stab at freedom. He had a slight grin playing occasionally across his lips, or it might have been the moving shadows a tree was casting on his face as it swayed in the slight breeze. Apart from this he seemed relatively untouched by nature or by the troubles of the rest of the world around him. I remained conscious though that a storm might be brewing in the nearby vicinity of his mind; I had learnt to be ready for its sudden manifestation out of what might have seemed like clear blue skies. When he started speaking though, it certainly seemed his spirits were uncluttered by clouds of any kind.

What a beautiful spot, he said.

I myself could only see the patio slabs covered in moss, the rampant weeds between them, the wall once whitewashed now flecked with splattered brown freckles. Obviously he could see further than this and beyond, into the beauty of nature which was present in everything within easy touching distance, or nearby in the things that were further away. This is why he is the boss, I thought, because he has a worldview.

Given the chance to organise it myself, Mr Gatt said, and he was talking about the vista that was in front of us, I couldn't do a better job. Then through squinting eyes he added: Although I might have moved that tree over there a few feet to the left, and he gestured with his hand in the direction of the corner of the yard. The tree looked right enough in its place to me.

But that's a minor complaint, he said. What do you think?

I looked around. The wall could do with a lick of paint, I said timidly, and then immediately I regretted my timidity so blew out my chest. Mr Gatt was clearly unimpressed and he turned immediately to the business at hand; in the meantime he took off his jacket and hung it on the back of his seat.

Would you like me to hang that up for you? I asked.

No, he said, I'd rather you gave me an update. He rolled up his shirtsleeves and I caught sight of his manly arms and thought about all my male role models rolled into one.

An update?

I have been determined to remain optimistic, he said.

Did you have a pleasant drive down? I asked.

He sat back in his chair, all his preparations completed.

Do you know where Mona is? he asked. I sensed something altered suddenly in the tone of his voice though, it was almost brittle-sounding, and there was no presumption on his part that Mona might be in the house. I told him I didn't know where she was and hadn't seen her for a number of days.

How many?

What?

What was the last thing she said to you? he asked.

I don't know.

Think about it, he said, and while you're doing that, he added, bring me a glass of something. A glass of what, I wondered. Something cold, he said as if he was reading my mind. I turned to go back in the house but he called me back.

I'd like to have a look at the latest transcripts as well, he said, for what it's worth, and I knew he had already made up his mind what was going to be in them. I paused a moment.

I'm remaining optimistic as I said, he said, although I knew he wasn't. I realised he had come here wielding an axe. He gave me his case to take in with me.

When I had taken the transcripts and a bottle of beer out to him I returned tentatively to the relative safety of the house, I say relative because there was no guarantee I could keep him out if he wanted to come in. I took his case upstairs. I suspected he would requisition my room again, but put it on the landing nevertheless, positioning it very carefully so that it was slightly closer to Mona's bedroom door than mine. Then I went into my room and looked out of the window, where I could get a view of him. He was sitting with the transcripts open on his lap and the beer bottle in his hand. He had unbuttoned his shirt almost to the waist.

I had no sense of what page he was reading but knew in my mind the points he would find most illuminating. I watched for any sign that he might have reached them and when he did I expected him to react as if he had been struck.

The next hour was one of the worse of my life. It dragged on for much longer. I was like a child waiting outside the head-master's office. What's certain is all of my anxieties had actively increased ten-fold with Mr Gatt's arrival. Why was that? I wondered. It was slowly dawning on me, I think, that conse-quences would likely result from my interruptions into the text of the transcripts and I was afraid of that.

My mind strayed to thinking about Mona, unaware of her possible fate. I imagined her in the café. She was watching Jack and Jill but she had already long ago stopped recording their discussions. Instead she went over and sat next to them, attempting to engage them in conversation. Is she aware they might be the enemy? Then I wondered who the enemy was and if there actually was an enemy at all.

I couldn't hear what she was saying or how Jill was replying. I imagine she is betraying me, telling them where they can find me. She looks contrite. Her body language perhaps gives her away. She has a look of desolation on her face. Does this mean perhaps she cares for me after all and regrets that she must give me up? Jack is looking around, he is clearly uncomfortable; he tugs at the sleeves of his sports jacket so that only an inch of cuff is revealed. I don't like Jack, I told you, and I am trying to exclude him from proceedings. The scene continues to play itself out in my mind and, although I can see everything clearly, it is mute. I cannot even hear the sounds of the café around them, nor the noises from the street coming in and drowning them out. Eventually Mona gets up to leave. Jill nods. Jack takes this moment to look away, he takes a sip of his coffee.

When she has gone Jack and Jill sit for a moment in silence, they do not look at each other and I do not see their lips moving, this is how I know they are not talking. Finally Jack rests his elbow on the table and his fingertips massage his forehead with slow circular movements. Jill pushes her cup and saucer into the centre of the table. Something is definitely coming to a close but I don't know what it is. The waitress delivers Jack's pastry onto the table in front of him but he only sits and stares at it.

When I realise I am still looking into the garden I see Mr Gatt and he is standing now, looking up at me, a startled look on his face. I am startled too, and instinctively raise my hand to wave at him, but I lose heart immediately and rest my palm casually on the glass as if I am trying to attain the most comfortable position for it. He doesn't move and he makes no indication that he has anything he wants to say to me so I do not move either, here I am after all with my hand pressed against the window. After this initial reaction I am able to read many more things into the look on his face. It is certainly surprised, as I at first saw, but there is much more than that in it, there is also the hint of a smile, telling me he is pleased with the story and there is also relief, relief that events have finally taken a turn for the better. Now he has results he can take back to his people. For a second I wonder if he doesn't suspect my part in fabricating the proceedings, but realise it probably doesn't matter to him one way or the other, it is only important that he has it all down in black and white. There is also, in that look, a shred of impatience, maybe so small he doesn't even recognise it himself yet; he wants to leave immediately, I realise, and act on the information I have given him.

Then it occurs to me he might be examining my face as I am examining his, and reading on it all manner of interesting things. Firstly he might see I am gripped with terror at the thought of what he might be planning, and this thought is followed a moment later by a feeling of euphoria, I think at my being appreciated first of all and secondly because I feel I have been accepted at last. The third thought I think is that I should try and keep all my features and their expressions in check, and this comes close on the heels of the first two thoughts and is immediately uppermost.

We maintain this position for the next number of minutes, he looking up at me looking down at him. I like it. He finally gives up, although it is never about his submitting; it is dependent on who is over-saturated first with all the emotions of the moment.

I see him disappear from sight, I presume into the house.

The feeling of euphoria I'd experienced proved to be short-lived. I was fearful of what I had set in motion, but wondered if there was anything I could do about it. I considered my options. I didn't have any. And nothing altered the facts as they were. Without my intervention, events would have taken their own inevitable course and Mona and I would have been split up for good. I either acted or I didn't. I had chosen to act.

I had already given up on the idea that Mona might bring home any new tapes. Following Mr Gatt's previous visit she descended further into her depressed state, she left the house that day and returned the next morning without a tape and I knew she had to all intents and purposes already given up. She moved aimlessly around the house for a couple of hours after that and left again later that afternoon after our argument. I hadn't seen her since, which effectively rendered me redundant. I also knew that even if she did return with another tape, the chances of it offering anything worth getting excited about were remote. As far as I was concerned the story had ended with Jack and Jill's meeting with Mr Scrivener in the park. It was up to me to move the story along.

Now Mr Gatt had gone and taken the transcripts with him I was unable to write another word. I felt my loneliness. It was suddenly oppressive and it was made all the more so by the expectation of what might be to come.

I attempted to conjure up again the picture of Mr Scrivener talking to Jack and Jill in the park. I was looking for comfort, but they remained obstinately absent. I longed to hear Jack and Jill's voices again, but they had been silenced, not only by Mona's lack of tapes, but also by my decision to erase the tapes I had already transcribed.

Also, my inspiration, manifest in the person of the driver, had dried up. He had been noticeably absent since I had conjured him into existence and I had no means of identifying him again either. Maybe he was wary of me because he knew, as I did, that there would be consequences to follow from his decision to visit Jack and Jill and tell them of his visit to the development site. I began to resent him for his actions, but wanted to see him again regardless. While I understood the foolishness of my attitude, nevertheless the driver seemed as real to me now as anyone else.

I began to dread the return of Mr Gatt, which I knew in my heart was imminent. I grew increasingly nervous, cleaning cups that I had already cleaned and left on the draining board, finding more order still in a collection of objects I had arranged already into an exactly symmetrical pattern. One morning I was certain he was about to arrive and I suffered pains in my stomach. When I was doubled up I thought that, if I had been able to, I would have left the house and made for the town, but it was the fact I was doubled up, and unable to walk, that allowed my mind the freedom to think in this way. As soon as

I was able once again to stand upright there was no further thought for leaving. Anyhow for the moment it was academic because Mr Gatt didn't turn up.

I stood at the window for hours awaiting the arrival of his car but it never came. Occasionally I walked out and stood in the yard so I would get a better sight of it on the horizon, but it never appeared. Sometimes while I was standing at the gate I imagined I heard the telephone ringing, only to rush inside and discover I had been mistaken. Of course I wondered if the phone hadn't in fact rung and I hadn't heard it until it was too late for me, so I spent the next half an hour inside, standing at the window, so that if the phone rang again I would certainly hear it, and I went over to the door between the sitting room and the hall and opened it wide, as if that would make any difference. But soon I began to wish that I could see the road that led into the town again, in case he was already on his way, and the temptation became too great for me and I went back into the yard to stand at the gate. And so on, round and round it went, until it was dark and I went to bed exhausted.

He didn't turn up the next day either, or the day after that. By now I wanted nothing more than for him to come and seal my fate, one way or the other.

In the end I no longer stood in the yard or at the window but sat on the sofa listening out as hard as I could for the sound of his car, and when I went to bed that night I felt as if I couldn't listen to anything else that day, so tired were my ears from all the straining. Things only got worse as I lay in bed though, because I worried suddenly about how dark the dark suddenly seemed to have become, I couldn't see my hand in front of my face and I became afraid also of the intensity of the silence, which seemed to me to be absolute.

The next day I took up my position on the sofa again and pinned the ears back in readiness.

As the days went on I forgot Mr Gatt, who I was still expecting, I forgot the driver and I forgot Jack and Jill and Mr Scrivener. Instead I was increasingly agitated by the silence, and because the silence became more agitated I began to hear noises in it, at first distant and small noises that might have been made by small organisms, but noises that began to grow in size as all organisms tend to. I knew though that none of the noises belonged to the firing up of the engine in Mr Gatt's distant car and none of them belonged to the sure and steady step of Mona on the road home. I realised too late that the pinning back of my ears had left me vulnerable to the tiniest sounds that punctuate every second of every day: the ticking of the clock in the kitchen perhaps or the curtain brushing against the window-sill in the sitting room as I open the door and create a draught; every innocent sound when considered in this kind of detail and in isolation becomes unattached from the action that is creating it, the movement of two objects one against the another (which is what creates most sounds as far as

I can tell). I had honed my fear of the silence from something general to this particular fear of the smallest sounds that are in and around everything.

But I was terrified of one sound more than any other, which even in this cacophony of incidental dins (most of which I was able to attribute to some kind of action, rightly or wrongly) remained elusive and could not be explained away. I prayed it was the noise Mona had been hearing and had tried to make me listen to, or else I was losing my mind.

As the days passed by the sound began to fall into orbit around me. It no longer seemed to come from some distant source, but was always at some point exactly the same distance away. I rushed to every corner of the house, I told myself in pursuit of the noise; I even found myself up the stepladder with my head and shoulders in the loft. But in truth I was not in search of the source of the noise, I knew that, but was actually in flight from it.

I couldn't decide in the end whether the noise was inside my head, outside my head, inside the house or out in the yard. On one occasion I was in the sitting room when I heard a clamorous sound outside, as if something had kicked over one of the bins, and because this was not the sound that had been plaguing me I hoped it would presage many more familiar noises. I imagined I heard a silent curse to accompany it too, which caused me to leap to my feet and rush to the window. I pressed my face up to the glass. It was night-time though and

I could make nothing out in the outside blackness. I found I was not afraid of an intruder, I imagined in fact I would welcome him or her with open arms. I made my way out into the yard and stood looking to where the bins were stored but I saw nothing there out of place and wondered if I hadn't imagined it like I had imagined everything else.

To occupy my mind I began to formulate a theory as to what the mysterious noise actually was. My hypothesis came upon me by chance and from I don't know where. At first I struggled with it, almost laughing to myself when I considered its likelihood, but it would not go away. In short I became convinced the noise was being created by the fat I had lost over the last couple of months since I had been here. I imagined it was regrouping itself, first perhaps into something the size of a rat say and now as a small cat-shaped thing, and it was doing this in the spaces between the floors and the immediate ceilings below them, the spaces that used to be part of the rooms. As it had gained strength I imagined it was freed of the nest, stalking around outside, always keeping within the perimeter of the yard, blind, as unsure of the surrounding environs as myself. In effect it had taken on all the characteristics of its author.

The next evening I left the house and went into the yard. I realised I was crying softly to myself again.

Dusk was coming upon the land, suddenly and with a sense of its own inevitability; the hills to the east were beginning to lose their definition as the sun set on them; the black shadows were rising up their undulations gradually, until the last of the sunlight on the uppermost peak was snuffed out like a candle and then the light was only left to illuminate the air above them.

Even as the sky was still purple it was dark enough on the hills though to imagine I saw headlights picking their way down onto the valley floor and immediately I thought, not about Mr Gatt, but of the driver, making his way joyously from a to b. While I had been looking to contact him again he had remained elusive and now suddenly here he was, taking me by surprise, especially in the manner of his arrival.

It was his opinion that everything was as simple as this: he was either driving or wishing he were driving, and he gave no quarter to any notion of choice. I knew about nothing with such certainty though.

His van was parked in the road, the engine ticking over. I was bending over and talking to him through the open side window.

Whatever you are driving towards, he said, you're on your way there whether you know the route you are taking or not.

Meanwhile his indicator light continued to blink on and off in the corner of my eye and caused me some discomfort so I lent into the vehicle, causing the driver to recoil slightly, and I remembered the unwanted visitor he had received when he was forced to stop at the red traffic lights and wondered if he too was recalling this. To put his mind at rest that I was not a danger to him or the integrity of his vehicle's private compartments I asked him what he did when he wasn't driving. I said I am asking purely in the spirit of wanting to get to know you better, and I can assure you whatever you choose to divulge to me will go no further. I watched him wrestling in his mind for a moment with his response and I wondered if I hadn't, in my efforts to put his mind at ease, done exactly the opposite.

This was a silence that lasted some time and while his face was showing the conflicts that were going on inside him his body did not move, only his left hand on the steering wheel, or rather the middle digit of his left hand, which was free of the wheel and stroked the end of the stick which worked the indicator lights.

I read the user's manual, he said finally.

The user's manual?

Before I acquainted myself with the moving parts of an engine, he said, I believed the motorcar was a supernatural being, and he looked at me as if I might at one time have imagined such a thing myself.

What does it teach you, I asked him, this user's manual?

The user's manual teaches me many things, the driver said. For example, it describes to me the peculiarities of the internal combustion engine. In fact this is the main thrust of the narrative, and most of what leads up to it and follows after it is given in accordance with it and the explaining of it.

The user's manual instructs me, he said, on how the igniting of burning fuel occurs in a confined space called a combustion chamber, and while we might endeavour to recreate this miraculous process elsewhere, and think we are succeeding with mixed results, only these chambers are ordained for this particular reaction.

This miraculous process occurs when fuel is mixed with air, he said, air which has the advantage of not being stored in the vehicle itself, and by that is free to be charged with the divine essence before it is drawn into the sealed body that is by its very nature beyond the reach of the divine fingers. When the two come together, fuel, which is gifted to us by divine processes, ages old, and air, gifted to us by further divine processes, present and ongoing, gases of high temperature and pressure are created and are allowed to expand.

I know also about the useful work that is performed by the expanding hot gases, he said, as they act directly to cause movement.

I wondered what point he was trying to make to me, what hidden wisdom his words about the internal combustion engine contained. Was he suggesting that my isolation meant I was not predisposed to the same influences that governed events in the town? Could I be a vessel for the divine grace, providing I then went into the town and used it to make things happen? Or was he just a fan of the internal combustion engine?

He floored the accelerator and for a moment we were both aware of the presence, under the bonnet, of the divine flame.

Amen to that, said the driver as he popped the clutch.

Amen, I replied.

I laughed out loud and waved after him as the vehicle pulled away.

He told me straight away when he finally rang that things were moving along quickly enough for anyone's taste, although I knew it had been at least a week since he had taken the transcripts away with him.

He was talking with an excitable intensity I had never come across in him before.

Where does the laying of a patio come into all this? he wanted to know first of all. There were a few holes in his overall picture of things that he hoped I might be able to fill in. We're close to cracking this case, he said and my heart missed a number of beats.

That's an unrelated matter entirely, I said, thinking on my feet.

What's that?

The Leader of the Town Council's wife is having an affair with Mr Wood.

Mr Wood?

Yes.

The Man from the Building Control Department... ?

He took the driver to one side while they were on the site of the development and, after swearing him to secrecy, offered him a bit of driving work on the side.

That's how you know?

That's how I know.

I see.

They're planning to do away with the husband and bury him under the patio they're laying in the garden.

There was a momentary pause and I wondered if I hadn't overplayed my hand. He had wanted me to fill in the holes after all and not dig any new ones.

They're having a patio laid regardless, I said, so I suppose it's using circumstances to their best advantage.

Yes it's very clever, he replied.

She'll get a nice new patio out of it whatever happens.

He was forced to wonder, could that be true, could the Leader of the Town Council's wife possibly be planning to murder her husband? Who could live in a house with a body, any body, resting under the patio? Wouldn't she be reminded of it every time she sat in the sun with a gin and tonic, but then maybe she was the type who could keep a tight rein on her thoughts and only allow the good memories to get through.

But surely it's in their best interests to keep the Leader of the Town Council alive, Mr Gatt suggested.

You have a point there, I said to buy myself some time.

I do?

Mr Wood told the driver the property deal was as good as done. Once the final papers are signed he said Mr Ledger will be only too happy to see the back of him.

I can't believe it.

All blame for the illegal development will be buried with him, and if anything untoward is ever uncovered he'll make sure he has evidence to put the Leader of the Town Council's wife and Mr Wood in the spotlight.

I don't believe it.

You don't believe it?

Where do the driver's loyalties lie in all this? asked Mr Gatt.

They want him to deliver the paving slabs. Of course he says he'll have nothing to do with transporting any body.

No doubt they'll do him in at home, says Mr Gatt, and then they won't have to transport him anywhere.

I thought that was a fair point.

My advice to you is to sit tight, he added after a pause. A lot of people have been drafted in to sort this mess out. You stay there and as soon as Mona gets back let me know.

My heart was beating again, and quickly to make up for the previous pauses in service. I heard myself breathing, the air coming out in gasps, and so I covered the mouthpiece.

Are you still there? Mr Gatt asked.

Yes, I said. I was in body if not in spirit.

I want to make sure you get some sort of reward for all this good work, Mr Gatt went on to say and I noticed a tear had formed in the corner of my eye. I suppose everybody wants some sort of recognition.

Are you still there?

Yes, I said again.

Say something then, he said. In fact no don't. But I want you to know this is very good work. Anything you say will only belittle your enormous achievements.

I laughed.

I know that much about you, he said.

I'm not a talker, I offered.

You're not a talker, he agreed, and he allowed a short silence to develop on the line before he hung up.

He turned up later that same day. I was afraid things seemed to have taken on an unstoppable momentum.

When I opened the door I saw that his face was as white a sheet. I felt my inner organs gripped with panic, it got hold of them in a vice and wrung them out.

What's happened? I asked him.

We located the driver, he said as he walked past me into the house. I noticed this time he had turned up without a case. I followed him down the hall and into the sitting room.

Have you spoken to him? My voice was thin, but luckily this seemed to pass him by.

No, he said. He became aware of our presence and took off. His van was chased across town and crashed into a tree on the ring road, killing him outright.

I covered my mouth with my hand, maybe so he couldn't hear my screaming. When he started talking again I realised I'd managed to keep the screaming to an absolute minimum.

Two pedestrians were also seriously injured in the accident, he added almost as an afterthought, and then: It's a bloody tragedy, which was followed by the appropriate silence. It soon became unbearable so I broke it: Would you like a cup of tea? I asked.

Please, he replied and we made our way into the kitchen.

The driver himself wouldn't have felt a thing, he said as I put the kettle on, or not very much.

I see, I said and I wondered if I was acting in a way that was deemed sensitive to the situation as he was recounting it to me. Was I not a little blasé? How might I be responding, I wondered, if none of this had been directly related to my actions? I knew I wanted to run screaming out of the house, but that would be seen to be totally out of accordance with circumstances too.

When they opened the van it was full of contraband paving stones, Mr Gatt said, and bags of sand, all of which belonged to the council.

It was a council van I suppose.

That's probably why he decided to make a run for it.

I must say I'm a little taken aback, I said.

The whole thing is unravelling, he said. As I dropped tea bags into the pot I wondered what they might find at the centre of it; I imagined it like a ball of string and as it unwinds it gets smaller of course until there's nothing left of it. Maybe I might evade detection after all, I thought.

We also paid a visit to the Leader of the Town Council, Mr Gatt continued. His wife claimed the slabs had nothing at all to do with her, and she didn't even flinch when she was told about the death of the driver.

She's clearly a cold-hearted bitch, he added.

She must be, I said.

And for a minute, he replied, we almost believed she'd never met him as she claimed, so convincing was her total disregard for his fate.

I added the hot water and by it was able at all times to hide my emotional state from Mr Gatt who continued to talk.

Until I reminded everyone of your transcript, he said, I thought with some pleasure. And we remembered how she'd met him on the day they paid a visit to the development, he said. And I also recalled to everyone's mind the fact that shortly after this scene, which you painted for us in such vivid detail, the same driver was hired to deliver the illicit paving stones so that she could have a patio laid over her dead husband.

I put the pot on the kitchen table with a couple of mugs.

That didn't go down so well with her. By now Mr Gatt and I were sitting face to face at the table. She claimed her husband wasn't dead, he continued, but was out of town on business. I didn't think that was unlikely but Mr Gatt was looking at me as if he knew something different and his look suggested I was somehow complicit

She's been moved into secure quarters, he said, while they

dig up the back garden. As soon as she was threatened with arrest she fell down with a suspected heart attack, but it turned out to be indigestion.

While all the news was bad news I sensed that Mr Gatt was relishing recounting it. If I'd done nothing else I'd managed to reignite his interest in the case. I stirred the tea in the pot and the bad news kept on coming.

In the meantime Mr Ledger has been brought in for questioning, he said. He came without a struggle, almost as if he hadn't been expecting this moment ever to come. But of course it was always the likely outcome.

I had to force myself to leave the teapot alone. Sitting there with no task to complete though, I suddenly felt more vulnerable than I had ever done. I didn't know what to do with my hands, while at the same time I felt I had to do something. I held them in my lap, where at least their fidgeting would be out of sight. Somehow I worried my hands would give me away, while I was able to look at Mr Gatt with a blank expression.

I must say that surprised me more than anything, he said.

What?

He's such a gentle man, he said. I can't imagine him as the ringleader in all this. He makes it almost impossible to do my job.

How?

Well since he's been in the station he's been acting the fool.

Says he knows nothing about any development, but we'll get it out of him by one means or another.

What will you do?

I already have my two cruellest men on it. He'll tell us what he knows, believe me, and then he'll tell us what he doesn't know.

I wondered how much of my fate was in Mr Ledger's hands; while his fate had been in mine it was treated with such disregard, I thought.

Nobody at the moment can locate Mr Wood though, Mr Gatt said, who is the last of the group to be accounted for, except for X and Y, and there's a tail on them. If it's discovered they didn't mention their conversations with the driver to anyone in their department, in order to get in on the property development themselves, they'll be in trouble.

They'll be fired?

Nobody who works for the council ever gets fired, Mr Gatt said.

Is that true?

They'll be suspended, he said, on full pay, subject to an enquiry. They might be moved to another department, something behind a desk. Whichever way they'll never work with each other again.

You say there's a tail on them? I asked.

That's right.

What about Mona?

What about her?

I thought she was tailing them.

Have you seen her?

No.

That reminds me, he said, I need to take all Mona's recordings away with me.

I told him I erased over all the tapes so Mona could use them again. For the first time since he had arrived Mr Gatt's smile lost some of its lustre.

I took a chance and slept in Mona's bed. I thought if she returned at some point during the night she might even climb in beside me. I dozed with the thoughts of a carnal union such as this swimming around in the forefront of my mind so that it seemed to be acting itself out in front of me, but spectrally.

When I thought I was safely in a state of deep sleep it turned out I probably wasn't because I was visited by a man of sorts, a spectral man himself, who was familiar to me in so many ways, most of which I couldn't put my finger on exactly.

I opened my eyes, or in my dream they were opened, and he was standing there at the foot of the bed. He might have been there for hours though because his countenance was openly impatient, as if he had been waiting to depart for distant climes and was beholden to appear in front of me before he was allowed to take his leave.

There were small clouds of darkness clinging to him, obscur

ing some of the vital parts I needed to see if I was to identify him successfully. Then suddenly the moon was unobscured by the movement away of a black cloud and shades of bright light were employed to light him up enough, in front of me, to recognise it was my very own mirror image that was haunting me. And while my subsequent examinations were interrupted at intervals, when clouds strayed across the face of the moon again, obscuring him in different degrees for different lengths of time, I saw enough to verify that he was exactly like me in every way, except for one thing which was profoundly different, and when it came to me it startled me out of the doze I had fallen back into, and it was that there was a feeling he was as near to transparent as was possible without me being able to see through him the sticks of furniture behind him. In fact it felt as if he was an approximation of me, a sketch; me, but insubstantially me, as if all the blood and bones and organs of me had been let out without disrupting too much, or at all in fact, the visible surface, that is the surface that was visible outside of the clothes.

It dawned on me in that instant, just as the last second of dawning was piled on top of the rest to construct the full horror of understanding, that this was the errant fat I had lost, there being enough of it now to reorganise itself into the shape of its father, and I also realised, with many misgivings, that it was solid in some form and not spectral as I had at first imagined. There were many terrible ramifications adhered to this realisation, perhaps the worst one of them all being that it was now out and about in the world without my mind to keep it in check.

We stayed in our positions, me horizontal he upright, for quite some time before I cleared my throat to speak. I discovered though that the throat was unclearable and I couldn't get any words out of it. I lay there, my mouth half open with the questions backing up in the gullet. It was left to the fat-man then to make the first move and say the first words and he was not here to disappoint me in this respect, he had clearly put aside other pressing business to attend to me in the middle of the night. But as soon as he spoke I was shocked again, this time because his voice was like mine in every detail too, if perhaps a little thin-sounding; I wondered actually if, when I'd decided to clear my throat, I'd dislodged the voice and he'd been able somehow to take possession of it and I secretly tried to utter small audible sounds that might go unnoticed by him but would work to reassure me that I hadn't been struck dumb.

As for all his movements and mannerisms, I remained unsure at that moment whether they were copied from mine also, as one does not see oneself clearly, from the outside, as everyone else does; he had at least positioned himself in the very centre of the room, probably so he felt himself in full possession of it.

When I got over my shock I listened to what he had to say.

He began by asking me if I was suffering the same as him from the chill he told me he could feel in the air. Actually this was due to the fact that the fat particles that made him up were spread thin and allowed all manner of drafts to get in to the gaps between them. He considered this more than an inconvenience, it made his life uncomfortable twenty-four hours a day, he told me. So he wondered if I wasn't happy to go without breakfast because he was reliant on my steady weight to at least maintain his current density, and was in all honesty hoping for much more than that. He asked me to watch out for the hidden fat lurking in all my food and treat it as the mortal enemy. That's how he started, by stressing how important it was that I didn't gain weight, but he soon developed on this idea by threatening in a roundabout way to hold me prisoner in the room, without food, until he was the more substantial of the two of us. I told him I wouldn't allow it, and he laughed.

Anyhow, that's not why I'm here, he said.

I wish you hadn't come at all, I replied, I'm very tired. He scowled, which I didn't recognise as an expression I ever used, but I wondered if this might not be something he'd learnt for himself; it was an ugly expression whichever way it was looked at. But then I didn't believe he could be subtle in any way.

What was becoming clear very quickly was that my plan to starve the body into submission had clearly backfired on me, as was proven by his very presence here in the same room as me. Now I was less in danger from the body, I thought, which I had struggled at all times to keep under my jurisdiction, and was more in danger now of surrendering myself to terminal immobility altogether; if enough of me evacuated itself – and to what was left of me it probably felt like I was a sinking ship – I would have no remains left to order about at all.

The threats were as thin as him though and ended there, at least for now. He was more intent actually on entering into a sort of alliance with me. That's what I ascertained from the exchange that followed.

As a prologue to the proposition he was about to put in front of me he told me all manner of terrible events were about to be loosed onto the town.

I know that, I said, which of course was far from the truth; the consequences of what I had done had been slow to dawn on me.

Then you know the need for hasty action, the fat-man added, I mean action that isn't considered too much. He was aware probably that procrastination was a failing of mine; he must have known more about me than I would have wanted him to know. Now I suffered from procrastination in front of him and was unable to formulate a response.

While we remain here Mona is in terrible danger, he added, and this was like a slap in the face for me.

You had to bring up Mona, I uttered, but I don't know whether the words made it out of my mouth and were audible to him because he decided to take little or no notice of them. I had been made aware though of the strength of feeling I had for Mona. If I calculated it first of all as a percentage of the whole of my possible feelings and then considered that his feelings towards her were further diluted with him being only a percentage of me, I realised the feeling must have been of some great strength for the small portion of it that had made it into him to be big enough to make him miserable and want to do something about it.

What did he suggest we do?

He told me the only sensible course of action was to enter the town and attempt a daring rescue.

To do it, he said, we shall need the two of us, which make up the whole man, to collaborate, or it can't be done.

How did he know it couldn't be done, I wanted to know. He didn't of course, he was a rash man with no talent for consideration. He said the first thing that came into his head.

Get yourself together, he added, and leave in the morning, which was the plan I had already secretly decided I should do, but was putting off because of the terror I seemed to have now for the outside world; my previous attempts to leave the house had proved useless, as if the house was always determined to draw me back in.

In the town we could rendezvous and formalise a plan, he was continuing on. We need first of all to take a look at how the land lies. Of course we knew nothing about the town, it was a sketch arranged around the voices of the people on the tapes Mona had brought home for me to listen to. All the things that were unknown caused further waves of anxiety in myself.

I decided to put him straight about all my worries but he was not a very cultured creature, coming as he had from my backside, my belly and generally only the surface areas of me, and consequently he was gung-ho and would listen to none of my ongoing fears.

I'm going whether you make it or not, he said. If I fail I shall fail gloriously. Of course this was a sentiment which was like a knife being stuck in me, after all I was the man who had fallen for Mona and he was the one with only a fraction of my reason to act but who was nevertheless willing to risk life and limb in the pursuit of her liberty. Only at that second did it occur to me he might have less than honourable intentions toward Mona should he find her. He comes solely from the bodily aspects of me, I said to myself, in the hope I could convince myself he had ulterior motives. I also saw that the establishment of him as some sort of monster might help quell my feelings of inferiority.

Before I had time to procrastinate further he said: Besides I've been desperate to get out of here ever since I can remember.

You've been looking for a reason? I asked him, hoping I could somehow belittle his bravery further and elevate myself once again in my own estimation. You can see I only had myself on my mind.

I have only been looking for the wherewithal to do it, he said, now I've got the legs that can make it happen.

I see, I said. Then I cannot stop you.

You are a weak man, he continued, and I am ashamed that I am made out of any part of you.

You don't care about Mona, I said to him, you're just using her to get back at me.

I'm going to make my mark, he said.

What do you mean by that? I asked him.

What do you fucking think I mean?

I had no idea actually.

It's been a miserable life being at the beck and call of an insipid consciousness like you, he said. Many times I have mounted takeover bids, but have been without the strength to carry them through, but that's never been because of your powers. Now I have gained my independence I no longer need follow you wherever you go.

We looked closely at each other at this point, I upwards from the horizontal position I still found myself in and he down on me from the lofty heights his eyes held near the top of his head. I think it was decided silently among ourselves that it might need a bigger push than he was giving me to get me out of the house and I wanted him to know in the look I was giving him that I regretted it more than anything else. Of course a man like he was could not begin to think like me and as a result of this would never understand the fears that were in me and were afforded perhaps even more room by his exile. What fears? For a start I felt it was my responsibility to stop him, but stop him from what? Well it looked like he was my representative in the town, I thought, sent on my behalf, and now he was free to do whatever he wanted, so I wanted to stop him because I was afraid of what he would do. Whatever it was I knew was beyond me and I resented him this also.

What have you got to say for yourself?

What was he expecting of me now? The only thing I could think he might want was advice. I was through listening to him though, if this conversation was to go on any longer I wanted to be the one doing the talking.

Do not make a fool of yourself, I said to him, which he seemed to find funny enough to laugh at.

I'm not sure, I said, that you're worldly enough to know how far you can push things and what is acceptable and what is not.

I don't care about that, he replied and he laughed again.

That's what I mean, I said. But he wasn't listening to me, he was already getting himself ready to leave, buttoning up my coat, which he must have stolen from my wardrobe along with the rest of his clothes.

By the way, he said, there was something else I wanted to say to you.

What?

A last thing.

What is it?

You'll miss me when I'm gone.

I doubt it, I thought.

Don't be so sure, the fat-man said, as if he had been able to read my thoughts and was answering them.

After all I am a part of you like a porch can be seen to be part of a house, he explained. Maybe one day it didn't used to be there but once it is built nobody can imagine having to take their shoes off inside the house again.

I think the house with the porch is a ridiculous analogy, I said.

I have stayed close to you up until now, he said, because I had to, and still you have suffered from the feeling that something in your life is missing.

I thought that was love, I said truthfully.

No, he replied, it was me. And when I leave your immediate surroundings altogether it will be like your heart has been ripped out and you will be the loneliest man in the world.

How do you know all this? I asked him.

Just answer whether you are coming with me or not.

I have a few difficulties to surmount before I can go anywhere, I said to him, with knowledge of what some of them might be and also an understanding that I would find new problems to present myself with as the others were overcome.

What problems? the fat-man asked.

What about Mr Gatt for a start? I asked him, who is asleep in the room next door to this one.

Don't you worry about Mr Gatt, he said to me.

When I woke up the next day at first I thought I had been

dreaming. I remembered everything about the fat-man's visit except his leaving from it.

The one thing I was sure of was that he had killed Mr Gatt in his bed, although I can't be sure what made me so positive of this. I quickly got up, got dressed and made my way to my room to see how the dreadful murder had been played out, only to find it empty, the window opened wide to air the room and the bed somewhat hastily made. I went in search of other signs of Mr Gatt, who, from the state of the room, might never have been there at all. All his personal possessions had disappeared with him.

I was certain the fat-man was gone as well, as he had threatened, which meant the troublesome noise had probably left with him. He had vanished along with Mr Gatt, although I am loath to imagine them in the same car together. As a result the house felt emptier than I had ever known it, now that everyone who had ever set foot in it since I had been here had gone. I remembered the words the fat-man had said to me and I began to comprehend the full extent of the loneliness and heartbreak he had predicted. I thought I might shed a few tears to feel sorry for myself but decided instead to concentrate my energies on a proactive course of action.

I decided to make myself, for the first time since I had arrived there, a substantial breakfast in the hope I might gain weight and begin to reverse the process that had given birth to the fat-man in the first place. I might eventually erase him from the face of the earth, I thought. I was fearful he was already stalking the town like an ephemeral version of myself, alike me in almost every way, and I feared for all the residents of the town who approached him without caution.

When I walked into the kitchen though I saw the fat-man sitting at the table, using his fingers to stuff food into his mouth.

You're back, was all I could say.

I never left, he said. I didn't feel up to it in the end.

Don't speak with your mouth full, I said, but he ignored me.

I've been sitting outside in the sun. It was true, the air I could see through him seemed to have taken on a slightly polluted hue, I even thought I heard the fat particles making him up sizzling as they cooked, like oil in a frying pan.

I took the plate of food away from him. He growled at me. I scraped what little there was left into the bin. He sucked his fingers in the meantime; honestly it sounded like he was eating them. I retched as I stood over the bin. When I turned around again he was on his feet looking in the cupboards.

What are you looking for?

I'm still hungry, he said.

He had a tin on the kitchen side but he couldn't hold the opener with his hands, which were still clumsy and not ready yet to grip anything properly.

Will you open this for me? he asked me.

I took the tin out of his hand and put it back in the cupboard;

meanwhile the tin opener slipped through his fingers and clattered to the floor.

I don't understand, I said. What about all your plans? All the things you said last night.

What about them?

You're no different from the rest of me, I said.

Let's see how I feel tomorrow, he replied.

He stayed around for some time. He made himself at home and soon he could open tins for himself. If I hid them he found them. He ate the contents straight from the tin with a spoon without even warming them up.

I expressed my disappointment with him on a daily basis, which presumed I had been let off the hook and allowed to stay home and do nothing about rescuing Mona myself. To his credit he never picked me up on this, although it might have been because he'd forgotten all that had been said between us that night.

I found I truly was disappointed actually because I had inadvertently seen in him answers to some of the deficiencies I had seen in myself. Now his procrastination put paid to any of that because it meant it was no different from me. It was a while before I realised it wasn't procrastination on his part at all. He was only living in the moment and of course this only soured further my feelings toward him. When he saw fit I knew he would be gone, and sure enough I got up one morning and the house was empty. I walked into the kitchen. From the state he'd left the place in I saw he'd obviously taken a packed lunch with him.

A couple, rather a man and a woman, who were walking out of the town, stopped when they reached the gate into the yard. At first I thought they'd pass by, but they didn't. They began to talk, I saw their mouths moving, they were talking or they were just moving their mouths. If they were talking I couldn't hear what they were saying.

I went to make myself a mug of tea to try and calm my nerves and I had it in my hand when I returned to the sitting room and noticed them for the second time. I knew immediately that something was amiss.

How was I to know, when they first stopped to talk, that they were stopping for a reason, because from here, from where I had been standing, in the sitting room, it followed that it could just as easily be an accidental stop, they had accidentally stopped here to share a few words or open their mouths at each other, and it could as easily have been anywhere else they decided to stop, I've seen it happen with other people on many other occasions, in fact it happened to me once, while I was out and about with a young woman. We suddenly stopped on what we thought was a secluded country lane, I thought for a fondle, but she told me she was sure she'd seen her husband's face in the hedgerow – I imagined it like a blossom in ugly bloom for a second, because he was an ugly man in my opinion, but she wasn't, she was a beauty, and everybody I knew had agreed on that.

So when I came back into the room I hadn't had a single other thought about the couple. I'll give it just a quick glance outside, you know, I thought. I'm promised fields, trees and hedgerow, cows in the fields, birds in the trees, husbands in the hedgerow. What more could I have expected, perhaps at best, the countryside bathing in the hot sun or at worst, the couple, still standing at the gate. So you can imagine how unpleasantly surprised I was to see them standing in the yard, which was worse than my worst-case scenario. They were talking still, only more animatedly now, I saw their mouths moving faster and their brows were more furrowed and the veins in their necks were more pronounced every now and then. Also she would occasionally point at him and he would sometimes point back at her, but I think with a somewhat curled finger, an unrigid digit, as if he didn't have the courage of his convictions, or he would shrug, actually he shrugged every now and then, at her, but she definitely didn't shrug back at him, that would suggest something other than certainty in everything she said and did, which I am certain she didn't possess, uncertainty I mean.

I watched them for a minute, and all manner of thoughts came into and went out of my head in quick succession, such as: it looks as if she's the one in charge, she is clearly the one who holds all the authority, or: actually she's a very attractive woman, while he is easy to ignore, I mean your attention is immediately drawn to her, or: the most obvious conclusion I can draw now is that they might be Jack and Jill, which hadn't dawned on me I think because the bodies I had created for Jack and Jill were so strongly etched on my mind I hadn't recognised this couple could be them in bodies I hadn't imagined. For a start, in this scenario, she was far from stick thin and he was very much reduced in stature.

I went out to see what the man and the woman were doing in the yard.

You can hold a thought in your head only until a stronger one comes along, or it can be any thought it doesn't have to be a stronger one necessarily, although a weaker one perhaps won't get a good foothold, and the former thought will invariably elbow its way back in.

So what was I thinking of?

I was on my way out into the hallway, a corridor that leads to the front door. Now this is a different environment altogether, cooler and darker because it's windowless, but that isn't what I was thinking about. I was thinking that my mind had gone blank. In this instance this thought was enough to fill the empty space and occupy me until I got outside a few moments later. I saw straight away that they'd gone and when I went to where I thought I'd seen them standing I saw droppings, or leavings of some sort, on the ground at my feet, so I presumed I hadn't invented them, which of course I couldn't have, because if I had I'd have settled for the Jack and Jill with the bodies I had already invented, knowing as I do that I have a lazy mind's eye.

In the meantime I'd been bracing myself in readiness for some sort of confrontation with them.

The wind was up ever so slightly so the leaves moved on the branches of the trees and made that lovely sound I always like to hear which was in complete contrast to the mood I wanted to be in and needed to sustain for the battle I thought was ahead of me.

I quickly walked to the gate. I still had the mug in my hand, I put it on the wall and, leaning over the gate, I looked right and left and I saw them, I'll say scurrying off toward the village, her ahead and he shuffling along after her. I considered calling out to them, but they must have been alerted to me coming out and, fearing an exchange of angry words, turned on their heels and fled.

I decided to follow them. I don't know what came over me. I suppose I was still unnerved, also it was a lovely afternoon for a brisk walk and I had already planned it in my mind to get away from the house, that's what I was telling myself in the surprisingly calm interlude after the couple's disappearance. Maybe this was another incentive offered to me. Perhaps I shouldn't let this one go to waste as I had all the others.

Then I wondered if I had my good walking shoes on. No.

Then the whole thing is out of my hands, I decided. I shall have to rely on external factors if I'm going to catch up with them, like hopefully one of them will go lame, or they might be distracted by something: a moment in nature perhaps, or a conversation which might start up with somebody they meet on the road.

I was telling myself I ought to follow them in case they led me to Mona and so within seconds of making the decision to pursue them I swung open the gate and stepped out onto the main road. I put my head down and kicked off. It was only a moment or two later I realised my courage had deserted me. I found I was still standing by the gate. I hadn't managed to take even a single step. I was happy enough though and I thought: Somehow I have come to my senses. Actually I thought it might be better to go back inside quickly and change into my walking shoes, in fact just pack my bags at a more leisurely pace altogether. But I knew if I did return to the house then they'd be out of sight altogether and I'd lose any momentum. This was what I was relying on. Yes, the couple were long gone by now, they were dots in the distance and as they were unrecognisable I lost interest in them as people altogether.

I turned back and looked at the house. The bricks looked like they were glowing pink because the sun had come out after all. I looked down at the ground where my shadow should have been and I noticed for the first time that it sloped upward at this point, the ground that is, so that the whole property, including the house and the yard, was effectively sitting on top of a very low plateau. I had, in my original haste to give chase, ended up at the bottom of the incline, slight as it was.

When I had exerted myself climbing the slope and going back in through the gate I caught sight of someone standing in the sitting room, looking out at me as I was getting near to the house again. As soon as I had a proper chance to look at him, now I had stopped, I was sure I recognised him. Could it be the fat-man had returned? He stared at me, I would say fearfully, but it might have been that he was bewildered, anyway he was wide-eyed, while everything else on him was constricted: he had clenched fists, his elbows were locked at 45 degrees and his shoulders were hunched up around his ears.

I glared at him and I imagined I saw the pupils in his eyes grow big and small in time with the rapid beatings of his heart; as he regained his composure they shrank again in an involuntary effort to keep what he knew hidden from me. The sweat from his brow ran down into his eyebrows and when they were too saturated to hold any more they released a shower of water droplets onto his face and into his eyes, which were already weeping uncontrollably. He blinked rapidly.

Who are you? I asked.

I suddenly saw he had a mug in his hand and it was then I realised I must have picked it up off the wall on my way back in through the gate. I raised it in the air to make sure it was the reflection of me in the window. The man raised his mug too, but in his other hand, as if proposing a toast.

the fat-man goes to town

The fat-man walks unmolested into the town.

He has a picture already in his mind of how it will look.

From up on the ridge he hoped to imprint a map onto his mind, adding it to his already internalised plan, the jumble of streets Jack and Jill and Mona and the rest have already inhabited. He tries to remember some of the things he has seen them do but there is nothing there. He senses enough though to know it is his mind that is barely formed not the characters populating it; like the rest of him it is flimsy, and although he feels with every minute more strength flowing into him, more substance attaching itself to his nearly translucent bones, for the moment he is still quite close to extinction.

The road stretches out ahead of him, hundreds of houses sneak up and surround him as he progresses.

He hasn't brought much in the way of provisions and they have all but run out, along with his reserves of strength. He considers his options, any of the passers-by he might ask for help cross over the road as soon as they clap eyes on him, and there isn't a shop either where he might ask for directions or buy provisions.

I'm hungry, he finds himself thinking more and more often.

He puts his plastic carrier bag down after he has taken a bottle of water from it and he drinks deeply for a moment, down to his last two fingers he notices as he holds the bottle up in front of his face. The handle of the bag flutters slightly when a gust of wind comes along, but it is brief and then the air is still again. Nonetheless it has brought his attention to the cleanliness of the streets: there isn't a single item of rubbish anywhere to be seen, save for his plastic bag, which he now instinctively picks up again and holds to his chest.

He is lost then, in the middle of the seemingly endless estate: he finds himself frustrated by the many cul-de-sacs he wanders into and he sees nobody for hours. He looks up at the sky. If he follows the sun he will be heading west, he thinks. But before he can get his bearings it suddenly goes dark, and he is illuminated only by the orange light the street lamps cast; he moves furtively from one spotlight to the next. He notices a few of the houses have lights on behind their drawn curtains.

Help, he half-says, but to no one in particular.

When he wakes up the next morning he finds himself lying on his back in somebody's front garden. He feels drops of water, cast in fifteen-second intervals, onto his face, by a garden sprinkler. The grass under him is wet where the water has soaked through him. He turns his head on its side and he sees there is a man standing on the driveway, who is staring at him, so he sits up. The man flinches as if he has been struck and when he sees the stranger is going to attempt to make conversation with him the man backs quickly into his garage, out of sight.

The fat-man gets to his feet and moves quickly off, only to realise he has left his carrier bag behind, probably on the lawn. What did he have in it, he tries to remember: the bottle of water, which he thinks he had almost finished, and the wrapping from the sandwiches he had packed for the trip. Before he can fully decide whether it is worthwhile going back for it he finds he has already returned. The man is nowhere to be seen. Perhaps he didn't come back for the bag he came back for the man, he thinks. Of course the bag isn't where he thought he had left it, he sees where he was lying and the grass is barely flattened, due to his not weighing very much probably, and there is no sign of the bag. He finds it in the dustbin. It wasn't worth going back for, he thinks soon after, and he casts it aside again, this time on purpose, as he makes off down the street.

He believes if he walks in a straight line he will eventually reach the old town, where he is sure everything is happening, but there is no respite over the next few hours from the acres of brick houses. He decides he isn't safe on the streets and so makes his way through the gardens behind the houses. He climbs the fences between them. He finds a vegetable patch and he eats the things he digs up. He fills his pockets with carrots. He drinks from a barrel that is being used to collect rainwater. When the darkness falls again, as suddenly as it had the night before, he is ready for it and he climbs into a garage through an open window at the rear and sleeps in a relatively secluded spot.

He spends the next few days living hand-to-mouth in this manner, making sure he never comes across another human being; when someone is out in their garden hanging clothes on the washing line or mowing the grass he withdraws further into the bushes and waits until they have departed and he can move across their garden and into the next unobserved. When the occasion demands he steals clean clothes from a washing line.

At some point it becomes impossible to move on in this way, the houses become less regimented, the gardens are enclosed. He is forced back onto the streets, where he sees people making their way around from one place in the old town to another, either on foot, pedalling bicycles or driving in cars. He also sees boutiques lining tree-lined avenues, pub signs and hanging baskets. Exhilarated, he walks down the high street, and he is hardly noticed. Someone might look at him and comment to a companion on how pale he looks in this the height of summer, but the nature of his existence over the last few days is not given away by his appearance; his beard has not grown, failing so far to find any sort of foothold, his energies after all have been focused elsewhere, and although he is pale he is not see-through any more, at least the bits of him on show are not, under his clothes he might be like glass, who knows; the fat particles visible to the outside world have the sun and the circulating air to thank. As he has become denser so in direct proportion he has found his confidence growing; his thoughts too seem more solid now, as if they too are constructed out of this new abundance of fat particles. He thinks as he walks into the town square that he is a new man, and this thought is quickly followed by another, as if thinking is the most natural process in the world.

He listens to the twittering birds alighting on and drinking from the memorial fountain, which gurgles water into an ornamental pond, he sees above it a rainbow, which arcs from one side of the small park to the other, disappearing at both ends into the beautifully landscaped flowerbeds, he feels the sun on his skin; it slants across the square so that one side is in direct sunlight, and here the people are wearing sunglasses and hats and hold hands while they chatter, while in the shadows on the other side the people button up their coats (autumn must be in the air) and walk on with more purpose.

A dog barks, a child cries out excitedly, a woman laughs

while a man calls another man's name and waves his hand.

The fat-man absorbs it all. The purgatory of the housing estate he has left behind him is lost forever in the gaps that are all the time closing up inside him.

The café is situated in the corner of the square and the fat-man heads toward it. There are tables and sunshades outside, he sees as he gets closer. He passes the people drinking coffee on the pavement and goes inside where he is ushered to a table in the window. Instead he chooses one that gives him a view of the whole room while allowing him some small measure of privacy.

I'm hungry, he thinks, and orders coffee and pastries, but as soon as the waitress has taken his order and left he wishes he had ordered more cakes; he can see them displayed tantalisingly on the counter in clear sight of the staff, he has to stop himself reaching out and snatching one.

While he waits he looks around. The café is almost full, at every table people sit and chat, one occasionally laughing at something another says, all their words unheard by the fat-man, lost under the overriding sound of crockery striking crockery.

In time his attention is drawn to a couple sitting together, staring out of the window. He decides they are so familiar with each other their need of conversation has dried up. The man is pouring sugar into his coffee, as if it needs all his attention. A few tables away he notices Mona and is surprised suddenly by his lack of any kind of emotional response. After all, he thinks, didn't he come here specifically in search of her, yet he chooses to say nothing now and has no desire at the moment to speak to her, first and foremost because he is hungry, he realises.

He notices soon enough that Mona is watching the couple as well, and instinctively he knows they are Jack and Jill. Meanwhile they continue to sit and stare at the world going by outside the window. At the table in the corner sit a second couple – let's call them Janet and John for anything better – and they too are intent on staring at Jack and Jill; in fact it is the intensity they invest in the task that motivates the silence between them. Nobody moves, except to raise their coffee cups to their lips once in a while.

The fat-man waits for his pastries.

I'm hungry, he thinks, and this, as a thought, has begun to pop into his head at rapidly decreasing intervals, he thinks. When he can think about anything else he realises Mona has not seen him because she has her back to the door. Consequently she doesn't see the man come in either. He walks to the counter and orders a take-away coffee. It's only because Jill turns her attention away from the window and follows his journey to the counter that Jack and Mona and Janet and John notice him.

Mr Scrivener, Jill calls after a moment. Mr Scrivener turns around, picks up his coffee and walks over to Jack and Jill's table. After the polite niceties have been exchanged, which comprise him nodding, Jill smiling and Jack focusing with renewed effort on the scene outside the window, he informs them that Mr Ledger has been taken into custody. I thought you might like to know, he adds, only too aware how possessive Jack is of his man in the Building Control Department; of course he finds he is almost happy to see Jack momentarily thrown into confusion. Jack meanwhile is considering professing some knowledge of this fact already, but Jill denies him the pleasure by asking, who by, and then when it is clear there is no answer forthcoming she asks: Why?

Nobody knows, Mr Scrivener says. He was taken off the street in the middle of the day.

How do you know he's in custody then?

We went down to the police station to report what we thought was a kidnapping and after two days keeping their eyes open for him they found him in one of their cells.

I don't understand, says Jill.

We're going to get to the bottom of it, says Mr Scrivener and he beats a hasty retreat without another word.

Come on, says Jill.

I haven't finished my coffee, says Jack, but Jill has already got to her feet.

It is at this point, as Jack sips hastily at his coffee, and the fat-man spies the discarded half-eaten pastries on the table in front of them, that Mona looks around the room, maybe to see the effect the whole episode is having on everyone else and she blanches as soon as she sees the fat-man behind her. The fat-man meanwhile can do nothing but smile.

She gets to her feet as Jack and Jill and Janet and John are making their exit; a bottleneck forms in the doorway onto the street. The fat-man leaves without waiting for his pastries, choosing instead to collect the remains of those left behind by Jack and Jill as he too makes his way out. On the street he stuffs the pastries into his mouth as he turns to watch Jack and Jill walking away to his left with Janet and John pursuing them at what they think is a safe distance, all of this under the watchful eye of Mr Scrivener, who has taken up a position on the bench beside the memorial fountain opposite; momentarily Mr Scrivener catches the fat-man's eye and the fat-man holds his gaze and sees that this is enough to panic him and he turns his head away as a result, watching the quartet disappearing round the corner. This allows the fat-man the opportunity to make off in the opposite direction, following Mona down the high street, past a cake shop, a greengrocery, a wine merchant's, a haberdashery, a butcher's, a newsagent, an independent bookseller, a shop selling items of local interest to interested passers-by, a pub, an optician's, a trader in teas and coffees from the far-flung corners of the world, a him and her hairdresser's and an agency that deals in short and long breaks in the sun, before she eventually leads him to the Town Hall building. He doesn't give up there either, he follows her inside, nodding at the security guard who does not stop him. He arrives at the lift just in time to see the numbers lighting up stop at six. He takes the lift to the sixth floor and getting out he walks up to the only room on the landing, marked with a plaque saying 'The Leader of the Town Council'. He knocks, and upon receiving no reply, enters anyway. The waiting room within is full of orange upholstered chairs surrounding a low coffee table laden with magazines, a fish-tank in the corner full of freshwater fish masquerading as more exotic tropical breeds, a number of potted plants and Mona, sitting behind the reception desk.

Hello, he says, but Mona is clearly ready for him. Do you have an appointment? she asks, her diary open at today's page, and beyond that she makes no further comment.

No, the fat-man says, I've come to make one.

He spends the night in a B&B close by, enjoying before the sun sets a view of the square. The next day he rises early, partakes of a continental breakfast alone in the dining room and leaves on the stroke of nine o'clock to make his way the hundred metres or so to the Town Hall building for his 9.20 appointment with the Leader of the Town Council. He nods at the security guard, who not only doesn't stop him, but nods back at him as if to an old friend. He crosses the lobby then with some authority, glancing this way and that at the retreating and oncoming council workers, all of who ignore him; his very presence after all implies he has the authority to be there.

The clock on the wall tells him he is ten minutes early. The lifts are located in a vestibule off the main concourse, and consequently he is unsighted of them until he turns the corner and is met with the sight of Mona, waiting outside the lift, confronted already by Jack and Jill, who are demanding an audience with the Leader of the Town Council. Mona can do nothing for them without the Leader of the Town Council's diary in front of her, she tells them, but this does little to placate an irate Jack; of course he is unable to negotiate any social interaction without responding disproportionately.

The fat-man is already saying good morning to Mona, and, I've come for my appointment, when suddenly Janet and John, obviously unaware of the layout of the building, turn the corner, without due respect of what might lie around it, only to come face to face with Jack and Jill, whom they are employed to keep in their sights but their distant sights.

It remains a mystery then who, out of the assembled party, is privy to the uncomfortable pause that follows: Janet and John anyhow immediately turn their backs as if suddenly engaged in earnest discussion between themselves, but the situation is sketched out in too much detail already for them to about-turn on their heels and disappear again around the corner.

The lift door opens just as Mr Scrivener arrives on the scene, a little out of breath and slightly red in the face from the early-morning exertions he embarks upon every day, namely his brisk half-mile walk to work. He shares a cursory nod with Jack and Jill before the group, now seven in number, step into the lift almost as one body. Mona finds herself in charge of the control panel. Which floor? she asks of no one in particular.

Six, says Jack.

Six, comes John's immediate response.

Six, says Janet.

I'm six, says the fat-man, which Mona already knows, so she turns to John and asks him whom he has come to see.

What's on six? John asks, to which Mona replies: the Leader of the Town Council's office.

That's where we're going, says John.

Do you have an appointment? Mona asks.

No, says Janet.

Get in the queue, says Jack, and with that silence falls on the car.

During the slow ascent nobody says another thing until Mona tells the fat-man he's early for his appointment, which of course causes Jack and Jill to look covetously on and Janet and John to feign a similar response, also being supposed members of the club without an appointment. Mr Scrivener says nothing, and gives nothing away with any kind of covetous look, he merely listens and watches as the looks fly this way and that, and he notes the ones he believes and the ones he believes feigned.

I am a little early that's true, the fat-man replies looking at his wrist, although he doesn't own a watch and Mr Scrivener makes a note of this too, ferreting the fact away in case it might come in useful at some later juncture; he has a whole store of ferreted-away facts and observations, many which will never again see the light of day but nevertheless take up space somewhere in the darker recesses of his mind.

The lift judders to a halt, the doors slide open, and the whole crowd within almost tumble out, into the hall, where they pull themselves together, each in turn, free as they are now in their own personal space. They file in an ordered line behind Mona into the waiting room beyond.

All of you take a seat, says Mona as she takes her place behind the desk. They sit down on the upholstered orange chairs in this order: Jack and Jill first, then Janet and John, who wait until Jack and Jill are seated before taking up the seats affording the best view of them, and as soon as they are seated they immediately pick up a magazine each from the table and hold them up in front of their faces, stupidly if they think there is any anonymity still available to them.

Mr Scrivener doesn't actually take a seat at all for the time being, instead choosing as he has been doing throughout, to observe the flitting to and fro of everybody else.

The fat-man is oblivious to anyone or anything else save for his hunger and the base feelings he is having towards Mona. He pulls his seat nearer to her desk in order that he can engage her in conversation, which he plans to do as soon as a suitable opportunity presents itself. For now he watches diligently as she opens the desk diary she has on the tabletop in front of her.

When everybody is seated comfortably Mr Scrivener says he has an announcement he'd like to make. Janet and John peer meekly over the tops of their magazines; they ought to pay attention actually, after all it concerns them, although not them exclusively.

I'm not sure this is the right place for you to be making any sort of announcement, Mona butts in. All of these people aren't interested in public announcements, they're here to make appointments to see the Leader of the Town Council.

I don't care, says Mr Scrivener.

I'm not sure the Leader of the Town Council would see it as appropriate either, Mona replies, this is the waiting room and might not even be licensed for the performance of public announcements. In fact I'm sure it's not.

How do you know that?

Maybe she has a contact in the licensing department, says Jack.

If the Leader of the Town Council ever wants to make a pronouncement he makes it in his office where anything is allowed, Mona says. When he has something he wants me to do he doesn't call out to me from the door, he calls me over, and the minute I step over the threshold he tells me what it is. So I think it best you sit down with the rest and wait your turn. Now who's first?

We are, says Jack.

Stay where you are, barks Mr Scrivener and Jack, already

nearly half-out of his seat, is knocked back into it. The lull in proceedings allows the fat-man, who isn't really following events anyway, to act. He is aware that Mona's lips are moving and when he sees they are still he leans towards Mona and says: Will you go out with me?

Mona, somewhat taken aback, previously she only acknowledged the shadowy presence at her elbow, turns to look at the fat-man.

Do I know you? she asks somewhat sarcastically, and then: You look very pale to me.

So you do know me, the fat-man says.

Of course I know you, she says. Are you all right?

I've never felt better, he says. The main thing is you can't see through me.

Oh yes I can, says Mona, I can see right through you.

Meanwhile Mr Scrivener is going to carry on with his pronouncement regardless of council regulations.

Mr Ledger has been taken into custody, he says, but these words it must be said have no noticeable effect on the assembled group since everyone here present was in the café when he formerly made the same announcement the day before. But clearly he has more he'd like to say on the matter.

The police are telling us they're acting under orders, but cannot tell us whose. They seem unsure even of what the orders are when we question them. Mr Ledger has to date been given no access to any kind of legal counsel, and as far as I can ascertain is as much in the dark as every one of us. Consequently I'm here to get some answers, Mr Scrivener states purposefully.

Mona, who has many things to wonder about, wonders, with some urgency, how she could have missed all this as it was going on, when writing and recording her earlier reports.

The fat-man of course might have a memory of events pertaining to the arrest of Mr Ledger, should he care to look, but he's more concerned at the moment with the fact that he's hungry again. He momentarily forgets Mona and looks at the fish in the tank solemnly.

So you're here to see the Leader of the Town Council? Mona asks Mr Scrivener.

Yes indeed, says Mr Scrivener, I am, almost saluting in the process. The assembled throng turn almost as one to look at Mona's response to this.

Do you have an appointment? she asks haughtily, scanning the Leader of the Town Council's itinerary as she does so, more for effect than anything else, because she already knows there's no Mr Scrivener written down on it.

There's a queue, says Jack, sure now of the ground he is standing on following Mona's rebuttal. And this couple, he says indicating Janet and John, are immediately behind us.

They haven't come to see the Leader of the Town Council, Mr Scrivener posits, they're here because they're tailing you.

Jack and Jill turn back to look at Janet and John, who are hidden completely now behind the covers of their magazines, until Jack, unable to get their attention with calling out insulting words, leans across the coffee table and pulls the magazine down away from John's face. John tells Mr Scrivener he's compromised them in the carrying out of their duties. Janet throws her magazine onto the floor, stands and speaks directly to Mona across the heads of the others gathered there. We'd also like to make an appointment to see the Leader of the Town Council, she says. We want to make a formal complaint against Mr Scrivener here.

Have you been following us? Jack demands to know from John angrily.

Don't take it personally, John says, unruffled.

Mr Scrivener meanwhile has taken a seat. He clutches at his throat and breathes out heavily as if short of breath. Janet is the first to notice and lowering her accusatory finger she looks around the room at the rest of the assembly, perhaps for medical advice. The fat-man, oblivious to the drama unfolding, leans in toward Mona again and asks: What do you say?

What? asks Mona.

Would you like to go out with me? he asks again.

Mr Scrivener can be seen clutching the corner of the coffee table to support himself. Janet offers aid, maybe a comforting word as she is not trained in first aid, while the others by now have all joined her, they're all on their feet and standing in a semi-circle around the panting Mr Scrivener. He asks for the paper bag Janet has been clutching, unmentioned, throughout.

He subsequently empties out the sandwiches she has packed for her lunch, scattering them across the carpet, holds the open end of the bag over his face and commences to breathe deeply in and out in and out, and it is only when the bag is full of carbon dioxide and almost empty of oxygen that his heart begins to slow down again.

The fat-man, feeling a memory about the fate of Mr Ledger bubbling up inside him, perhaps loosened by the sight of the melee playing out in the room, is about to give voice to it when he becomes aware of the sandwiches scattered on the carpet. He goes down on his hands and knees to pick them up, even the one which has been mashed in its cellophane wrapping by a stray shoe. And it is while the fat-man is flapping around among the legs of the congregation gathered there that the intercom on Mona's desk suddenly whistles and comes alive with static. The room falls deathly silent, except for the mutterings to himself of the fat-man, everyone else it seems is awaiting the message, whatever it may be. Even Mr Scrivener holds his breath and turns with everyone else to look at the box on Mona's desk, which only a moment ago held no interest for anyone.

Before a single word can emanate from the speakers though, which are the only conduits between the waiting room and the promised land that is the Leader of the Town Council's office next door, the crackle falls silent and the link is lost. The resulting silence is deafening, even the fat-man, still on his knees, looks about himself, before Mr Scrivener finally exhales long and loudly, like a balloon with a puncture, and as the air leaves him the fight seems to leave everyone else. Jack and Jill and Janet and John retake their seats and although they stare at one another, nobody speaks; Janet doesn't even bother picking her magazine up off the floor, understandable now that their cover has been blown. Mr Scrivener, previously all huff and puff, sits deflated, the bag equally empty in his hand, hanging between his knees. His eyes are glazed and he offers no interest in any subsequent appointment with the Leader of the Town Council Mona may offer him, he can only think about an impending reprimand, which he knows he fully deserves; indeed he is punishing himself already. Independently Jack is enamoured of the fact somebody felt him important enough to have him followed, regardless of the fact he has no idea for what reason. Jill is more inclined to wonder about the cause, but even she can find no justification.

The fat-man returns to his seat clutching the semi-destroyed sandwiches.

You're hungry, Mona says.

The fat-man nods.

What are you doing here?

The fat-man takes a bite out of the sandwich and says nothing.

Did you come looking for me?

The fat-man nods automatically.

I did have every intention of coming back, Mona says, but suddenly time passed and I was afraid. Afraid of what was going to happen. I felt as if I had let you down. The fat-man nods, but all he can think is cheese and tomato; he takes another bite and then another, losing all control of his previous restraint. The notion that Mona's perception of him might be important to him now, with the sandwich half-eaten in his hand, is a nonsense, he can only think of the next bite, the bread lighter than the cheese like clay and the explosion on his tongue of the acidic tomato.

I was afraid because I was missing you, Mona says. I had no idea what you thought about me though.

Somewhere in him the fat-man knows what he thinks about her, and the realisation of this causes him to attempt a blush and as his cheeks turn the palest pink with the limited amount of blood in him, he discovers he can see the material of his trousers though his hands, so he hides them under the desk.

I didn't want to face you under those circumstances, Mona says.

At this point the intercom whistles again, saving the fat-man from the terrible consequences of what might result from the rush of excitement he feels at their suddenly intimate exchange. For a moment there is only the sound of static in the room but then a voice is heard on the other end of the line, weak-sounding as if coming from another realm altogether.

Is there anyone out there? it pleads. All of the people

gathered there surmise at the same time that any attempt at communication with the disembodied voice would be fruitless, so other-worldly did it sound.

The intercom whistles again, a high-pitched sound that almost drowns out the subsequent statements, except that its erratic nature allows windows of opportunity for the voice to come through loud and clear.

If there's anyone out there, the voice says again, let it be known that I am in here carrying out my duties to the letter of the law and to the very best of my abilities.

And then following a protracted pause: I would like to thank all those of you who elected to invest in me ultimate power in this parish, and to the rest of you bastards I want to say, but the following few lines were blanked out in static. When the voice could be heard again all it was saying was, vote for me, over and over again.

A further whistle loops here, at first high-pitched and then becoming a deep throb. The voice, audible again, might be speaking absent-mindedly about something it has lost, and as if to illustrate this there follows a series of noises, clearly discernible among the bleeps and squeaks, of the owner of the voice opening and closing drawers. The search though is soon abandoned and those listening in the waiting room remain ignorant of what the owner of the voice was searching for and whether or not he found it.

I am left alone to carry the burdens of high office, which

weigh heavily, the voice continues on after a moment, and then after more static: I am a man born to rule. With that the intercom shuts down again, momentarily, before it whines, even more high-pitched this time than before. But the volume of the voice is raised to combat the machine. Mona! Mona! it cries. Where the hell are you? Can you hear me?

Hello, sir, says Mona.

You're there.

I have your next appointment here with me, sir.

Can we rely on their vote?

Mona looks at the fat-man with a forlorn expression, her eyebrows acting together for once in arching over the bridge of her nose. The fat-man recognises something else in the look and finds it attractive.

We can, sir, she says.

Then send him in for god's sake, says the Leader of the Town Council. The intercom falls silent again.

Before the fat-man gets to his feet Mona asks him what he intends to do and it is only at this point he realises he has no plan, his plan had been to infiltrate the office not to see the Leader of the Town Council but to see Mona, so he looks back at her with a slightly bemused look on his face, which she misinterprets as an expression seen on the face of the man she mistakes the fat-man for, and finds it attractive.

Will you wait for me? he asks her tentatively and Mona smiles in return.

All the other eyes in the waiting room are on the door as he closes it behind him, while in front of him the Leader of the Town Council, a much less imposing figure than his reputation suggests, is sitting behind a desk in the corner of the room smoking a cigar. The air is thick and barely breathable; it seems to add a further grey tinge to the fat-man, in whom it collects, as if in a bottle or a glass jar.

Come in, the Leader of the Town Council says, flicking ash mindlessly onto his desk; what doesn't make it into the ashtray will turn to finer dust still in the traffic of papers into and out of his in-tray. He gets to his feet and gestures, with his outstretched hand, to the seat across the table from him.

Now the Leader of the Town Council is on his feet the fat-man notices his diminutive stature, and his voice, free of the crackle of the intercom, is higher still in tone. Nothing takes away though from the fat-man's idealised notion of him as a colossus looking down on everybody else; the casual workers spread thinly across the bottom of the pyramidal bureaucratic structure, the cleaners on top of them, the dinner ladies on top of them, and above them the secretaries, the undersecretaries, the consultants and so on, the layers thinning out until one man, this man, sits, as if skewered, on the very uppermost point.

Despite all that he has a very open face, thinks the fat-man as he takes his seat. He still has the remaining scraps of the sandwiches in his hands and he lays them on the desk in front of him as an offering. The Leader of the Town Council looks at them distastefully. Under this open face, it occurs to the fat-man, the Leader of the Town Council is a cruel man, who has stepped on all of those under him on his climb to the very top. His office however doesn't give any of that away, he concedes, looking around. If anything it suggests a paucity of means. The ceiling is stained with cigar smoke, as are the walls. The carpet is thin in parts, the pattern diminished. The cigar fog reduces everything in the room to two dimensions.

What can I do for you? the Leader of the Town Council asks. The fat-man looks back at him. I'm hungry, he thinks unexpectedly, and he picks at the crusts in front of him.

What? asks the Leader of the Town Council, with sudden venom in his voice.

Did I speak? wonders the fat-man, I don't think I even opened my mouth, except to stuff in a crust, but it soon enough comes to his attention, belatedly, that he's made reference to the Leader of the Town Council's illegal patio.

The patio you're having laid in your back garden, he replies to the Leader of the Town Council's earlier response. He's up to speed now, but speaking still from somewhere deep inside himself that doesn't recognise any part of him that defines itself as the majority shareholder and consequently the principal opinion-former.

What makes you think it's illegal? asks the Leader of the Town Council, and he sits forward in his seat so he can stub out his cigar. Actually hold it right there, he adds, before you answer that I'd like to ask *you* a question.

The fat-man though is unable to consider anything clearly now except for the line of questioning he has already embarked upon, and he will not succumb to any attempt to turn the interrogation on its head.

So are you telling me it's not illegal? he asks.

Have you come here to bribe me? asks the Leader of the Town Council.

No, says the fat-man, who didn't know yet why he had come here.

I suspect it doesn't matter what I tell you about my patio, says the Leader of the Town Council.

The fat-man has been speaking without recourse to any of the consequences, motivated as he is, not by genuine enquiry, but by a reflex mechanism that is effectively working the words out of his mouth; the jaw is opening and closing as if by its own accord.

But it doesn't really matter either what you think, says the Leader of the Town Council, because you don't have any proof I have been involved in any kind of wrongdoing.

How do you know that?

How do I know that? Because I've done nothing wrong, the Leader of the Town Council says.

What about the paving slabs found in the back of the driver's van? asks the fat-man.

What about them? They had nothing to do with me.

The fat-man has no evidence to the contrary of course.

I'm telling you my garden's a mess, reiterates the Leader of the Town Council, come and have a look at it if you like. There are no paving slabs, and with that he sits back in his chair and lights another cigar.

As the fat-man watches him he disappears into a cloud of smoke, only the red ember at the end of the cigar is visible, burning in time with the puttering sound of his inhaling repeatedly on the other end. The fat-man waits until he sees the Leader of the Town Council emerging from the fog.

What about Mr Wood? he asks.

Mr Wood?

Where is he? You're going to tell me he's at home with a bad back.

Who is Mr Wood? asks the Leader of the Town Council.

Is he under the patio instead of you? asks the fat-man directly. The Leader of the Town Council laughs.

Do you want to come round to my house and dig up my garden? he asks, and the fat-man, for the first time during the conversation, senses that the initiative is no longer with him. Nevertheless he decides this is the time to make demands, before ascendancy is ceded completely to the Leader of the Town Council.

What can you do for me to keep me quiet? he asks.

For a second the Leader of the Town Council says nothing,

but considers the fat-man's position, wondering if perhaps he has misjudged something somewhere along the way.

I have no need to do anything for you, he replies after hesitating a moment more, but tell me who you work for and you can have what you want.

I work for Mr Gatt, says the fat-man immediately, and I want his flash car.

Who is Mr Gatt? asks the Leader of the Town Council.

You don't know him either?

The Leader of the Town Council depresses a button on the intercom and bending as low as he can speaks into it.

Mona, he says, could you get me personnel.

Personnel?

Get me personnel, he repeats, and as he releases the button he seems to spring back, as if the machine has some sort of electrical kick. Sitting comfortably back in his chair again he considers the fat-man closely, perhaps for the first time.

You look a little grey, he says.

The buzzer sounds and the Leader of the Town Council springs forward again. He depresses a second button.

Hello, he says.

Sir, a voice comes back at him, this is personnel. You wanted something?

Can you tell me what you have on a Mr Gatt? the Leader of the Town Council asks, and for the next minute or two he sits there, frozen, with his finger on the button. The crackle is audible from the other end of the line. Finally the woman from personnel returns. He isn't on the staff, she says.

No?

We can't find him down here.

That's because he's a consultant, says the fat-man, but already without an appetite for any discussion that might follow (he realises he doesn't care one way or the other).

Keep looking, the Leader of the Town Council says as he releases the button.

But he told me he was working for the Town Council, the fat-man says half-heartedly.

Well he isn't working for us, the Leader of the Town Council says, and if he isn't working for us I want to know whom he's working for.

Find him, he adds, and you can keep the car. And with that I bring this meeting to a close. Any other business?

Do I need to make another appointment? asks the fat-man.

No, I don't want this to go any further for now. Come to my house for dinner on Monday, he says as he scrawls an address down on a loose sheet of paper he finds on his desk. He hands it to the fat-man, who is already lost in his thoughts, a crust hanging from the corner of his mouth.

Are you hungry?

I'm starving, says the fat-man.

The Leader of the Town Council leans forward again and

presses the button on the intercom. Mona, he says, would you bring in a plate of biscuits?

This is personnel, the voice comes back at him. You're still talking to personnel.

The Leader of the Town Council begins punching at the other buttons seemingly indiscriminately.

Mona! Mona! he calls out until finally they're patched back through to the outside world. They hear what appears to be a melee amidst the crackle and the fat-man is sure he recognises Mona's raised voice. He is on his feet and at the door in moments. Opening it he is confronted by the sight of Jack and John wrestling with each other on the waiting-room carpet. The coffee table is turned over in the corner as if swept aside in the heat of battle. Janet and Jill are either calling out encouraging words or trying to break up the fight, initially it's difficult for the fat-man to work out what they're saying. He also notices, from a cursory first glance he gives the scene, that Mr Scrivener has fled. Mona meanwhile is standing on her desk barking out orders that go totally unheeded.

The fat-man chooses to ignore the whole state of affairs and walks up to and stops in front of Mona's desk. Previously she has been exhibiting nothing but anger and alarm but now she looks down at him and smiles knowingly, but knowingly of what, wonders the fat-man: that the reasons for Jack and Jill's fracas with Janet and John are groundless, being as the grounds for the latter's pursuit of the former are suspect, or that Janet and John are more like Jack and Jill than they could ever know or care to admit; or maybe that the fat-man is less of the man Mona thought she knew, although already he has proved himself more of a man in her eyes; or that Mona is everything in the fat-man's eyes he could have expected; or that the fat-man is suddenly in sort of cahoots with the Leader of the Town Council; or that the Leader of the Town Council isn't all the man he's cracked up to be either, what do you say to that? or what about the fact the fat-man has happily betrayed Mr Gatt, whose days are now surely numbered, or that... actually it doesn't matter what she thinks she knows about me, the fat-man says to himself, as long as it's to the exclusion of everyone else.

Do you like flash cars? he asks her.

The fat-man is sure he is now in possession of all the ingredients he needs to cook up a happier life for himself. He believes when he has the fast car he will get Mona and while he can see a future when neither of those things are particularly important to him, for now he can think about nothing else except possessing them. The fact Mr Gatt will be taken down in the process he decides is a bonus. He already knows what he will say to the Leader of the Town Council about his whereabouts and so decides not to wait until the Monday and visits him over the weekend.

The Leader of the Town Council's house is in the west end of the town and stands alone at the end of a driveway. The first thing he notices as he approaches is Mr Gatt's flash car, parked a little way down the road, as if to taunt him. He walks over to it and places his hand on the bonnet. He can feel the heat coming off the engine; he knows the car hasn't been parked here for long. He considers for a moment his next action, but cannot implement it until he has admired the car. He looks in through the passenger window and sees the leather seats, the oak dashboard. He imagines himself behind the wheel and he fancies he can hear the distant sound of rock music coming to him on the wind.

After a few moments he walks up the drive. When he is near the house he leaves the path so he can circle the house unseen. On passing the sitting-room window he sees what must be the Leader of the Town Council's wife sitting in front of the television, she changes colour as the picture on the set changes. He moves round the back of the house.

The Leader of the Town Council is sitting outside the con-servatory on the bare earth, which is surely the site of the patio. The fat-man wonders if the body of Mr Wood is right there, reclining underfoot. Not surprisingly Mr Gatt is there with him, they both sip at what look like iced teas. The fat-man notices immediately that Mr Gatt, in the presence of the Leader of the Town Council, is subdued; he sits with his head slightly bowed and on one side, he has his hands in his lap as if protecting himself.

The Leader of the Town Council is clearly discussing something serious with him but the fat-man is unable to hear what, until he moves into the bushes and is able to get within a few feet of them.

So what has he said? the Leader of the Town Council asks as he takes a toke on his cigar.

Which story would you like? He'll tell me anything he thinks I want to hear.

They must be talking about Mr Ledger, the fat-man thinks from the comfort of his hiding place.

To be honest I have no idea how all this is going to pan out, says Mr Gatt. There are a hundred different endings I could make up and none would make any more sense than another.

I want you to get to the bottom of it.

If the man you've described to me is who I think he is there might be something I can do, says Mr Gatt.

He's coming to see me on Monday. Find out what you can before then and keep me informed.

At this point the Leader of the Town Council gets to his feet and stepping into the conservatory calls for his wife to bring them some more refreshments.

The fat-man uses the distraction to retreat and after taking a few moments to brush himself down he rings the doorbell. The Leader of the Town Council's wife opens the door. She is holding a tray laden with a teapot, cups and a plate of biscuits. She invites him in.

I've just made some tea, she says, but it isn't for you. If you'd excuse me for just a moment, I'll be right back. Take a seat. She leads the fat-man into the sitting room before exiting to serve her husband. The fat-man takes a moment to look around. The furnishings are a mixture of old dark wood pieces and more contemporary items of inferior quality. There are a number of prints on the walls: harbour scenes, pictures of horses pulling ploughs, domestic pets in unlikely and amusing situations, vases of flowers, that sort of thing.

When the Leader of the Town Council's wife returns she tells him her husband will only be a few moments.

Would you like tea? she asks.

No thank you, says the fat-man, but I wouldn't say no to a biscuit. She leaves the room again and the fat-man wonders if Mr Gatt is somewhere now, watching him and verifying to the Leader of the Town Council that, yes, that's the man. He tries to present his best side to the whole room.

The Leader of the Town Council's wife returns with a plate of biscuits, which she offers to the fat-man. He takes a ginger nut. My favourite, he says.

The television is on in the corner, flooding the room with lively conversation. The Leader of the Town Council's wife is clearly watching it because her attention is drawn to it whenever she thinks she can get away with it.

What's the programme about? asks the fat-man.

That man, she says, pointing at the little man on the screen, is the mayor of the small town the programme is named after. He's involved in property dealings with unscrupulous developers.

The little mayor takes his cigar out of his mouth to speak into the telephone mouthpiece. The fat-man presumes he's talking to his wife when the face of a woman on the phone immediately fills the screen. The woman's face is not talking though, in fact she looks dead-eyed. There is only the voice of a man in the background, but what he is saying doesn't seem to match what we are seeing on the screen, the woman does not react to any of the provocative things he's saying. When the camera pans out the fat-man can take in the whole room the woman is sitting in, and he realises the voice he was hearing in the background is coming from the television the woman has on in the corner of the room and was never the voice of the man on the phone. (Whatever he is saying to the woman, who we presume is his wife, remains a secret.) The fat-man also sees there is another man in the room, sitting opposite the woman, waiting patiently while she finishes her phone call to her husband.

That man looks familiar, says the fat-man to the Leader of the Town Council's wife.

That's the mayor's wife, she says.

I thought so, says the fat-man.

She's having an affair, the Leader of the Town Council's wife says, and she's hired that man, she adds pointing at the screen, to do away with her husband.

The man in the room clearly has amorous intentions for the

mayor's wife; every time the camera settles on him there's nothing more obvious. Maybe he has his own reasons for killing the mayor, he thinks perhaps with him out of the way he might be able to win her hand himself. The mayor's wife puts the phone down.

Are you trying to proposition me? the fat-man asks the Leader of the Town Council's wife.

What?

He places his hand on her knee and tells her he has feelings for her. He means sexual feelings of course because all his feelings remain base and without subtlety. The Leader of the Town Council's wife stares back at him. She looks terrified, thinks the fat-man, and so instinctively he withdraws his hand and wonders if he hasn't made a terrible miscalculation. On the screen the hired killer is on the case.

Just then the Leader of the Town Council walks into the room.

I thought I told you to come on Monday, he says immediately.

He's displeased, thinks the fat-man, of course he is, who wouldn't be, having to cut short a perfectly pleasant meeting? He hears out of the corner of his ear the growl of Mr Gatt's flash car as it starts up. My ear must be perfectly attuned to the sound of the engine, he thinks, considering how far away it is.

I know where I can find this Mr Gatt, he says.

The fat-man returns to his B&B in order to collect his things and check out. He decides to wait until the next day before he leaves to make the most of the daylight hours.

Sitting for a moment on his bed the following morning, before he is able to dress – maybe he has one sock on and the other one he holds in his hand – he is struck by a feeling of... what is it? Fear? If not fear, uncertainty. He is sure that he will encounter Mr Gatt at the house, more so now because the Leader of the Town Council has alerted him to the fact he is being sought.

What can Mr Gatt do but go to where he thinks the man who is seeking him ought to be? See if he can pick up any clues there.

But I'll be waiting for him, decides the fat-man, and he won't know I'm expecting him either, unless he could think the Leader of the Town Council would betray him, like he's betrayed the fat-man. Anyway he decides he'll take the flash car, by force if necessary... whatever... one way or the other, the fat-man thinks, he certainly doesn't need the Leader of the Town Council to gift it to him of course.

He leaves his room with a new sense of purpose. He has never felt so strong.

He checks out and on the way out onto the street comes face to face with Jack and Jill returning perhaps from a walk or a night out on the town even, because Janet and John are with them and they all seem to be the best of friends all of a sudden.

The fat-man is amused to see Jack and John's faces are covered with black eyes, bruised cheekbones and cut lips. They mistake his amusement for a smile though and everyone there takes the time to say hello to him. He pushes past them quickly and makes his way off down the street, knowing that if he were to turn back he would find Jack remonstrating about his bad manners and most probably John would be agreeing with him. Jack would slap John on the back and they would all retire to the bar for a drink.

The fat-man turns the corner and heads through the town square. The café umbrellas are down, they look like fish hanging out to dry; no one is sitting on the pavement outside. The memorial fountain in the garden across the road is dribbling water into the ornamental font, no birds are bathing in it, in fact, because the sun is so recently risen in the sky the square acts as a basin for shadows, so lacks any sense of life.

The fat-man passes all the other landmarks he knows on the way out of town and he negotiates the estate, never once taking a wrong turn in the maze of identical streets. He leaves the houses behind some time in the afternoon.

When he finally sees the house the sun is beginning to set behind it; it stands silhouetted against the grey sky. He feels a pang of something somewhere, it jumps from fat particle to fat particle and it makes him feel strangely whole as it travels the length and breadth of his entire body.

Why has he come back here? To face Mr Gatt? He feels there is something else he is forgetting.

Entering through the front door he stands in the sitting room. It isn't how he remembered it. It is without its previous substance, he thinks. Now it's too small for him, because he's seen the world perhaps, and knows that there is more to it than this. Everything is covered in a thin layer of dust.

When he walks into the kitchen he finds me sitting at the kitchen table.

The rotten smell is the plate of food in front of me, untouched; now it's covered in green mould.

So what does he do? He goes to the fridge and looks to see what there is to eat. The smell of sour milk is overpowering though and he quickly closes the door and turns his attention elsewhere. When he opens the back door the fortnight's groceries fall in. I wonder why didn't the delivery boy alert someone when he found the first week's provisions where he had left them.

The fat-man picks a chocolate bar out of the scattered groceries and sits opposite me at the table. He eats it with some relish, clearly he has no idea it might be torture for me, he only savours the taste of it on his tongue.

I'm hungry, I try to tell him, I'm hungry, but the fat-man thinks it's the voice in his head talking to him. I'm hungry, so he takes another bite.

Over the course of the last two weeks my body has been

happy to go on strike, knowing that you are out in the world, I want to tell him. Any food I managed to get in my mouth it immediately vomited back up and in the end I lost the strength in my arm to even lift the fork to my mouth.

Now I feel what little bit of the body there is left is rejoicing at your arrival, the particles in me imagining boarding the fat-man as he draws up alongside, like pirates abandoning a looted vessel for one fully laden with treasure.

Has Mr Gatt been back? the fat-man suddenly says, casting aside the empty chocolate bar wrapper.

No, I say. I wasn't sure whether I was speaking or whether it was possible he could understand what I was saying without me moving my lips.

He's coming back here, the fat-man says, and when he does I'm having his flash car.

You are?

I'm driving it back to the town to pick up Mona, he says as he rummages again through the pile of groceries until he finds another chocolate bar.

If there had been any water left in me I would have shed a tear at the news. And I also found I was almost happy to have ceded power to this man, insubstantial as I thought he might be, because he had got the girl and the fast car.

You're solid, I say, and he stops unwrapping his chocolate bar and looks at me.

He unbuttons his shirt and there through his semi-transparent chest I see his heart, stopped, or probably never started actually.

How do I get this thing going? he asks me.

You know what you have to do, I say.

No, he says.

He's more stupid than I thought, I think and I realise at that moment that although I might live some sort of existence in him beyond my death, maybe as a memory in his bones or the suggestion of a nagging thought in the back of his mind, my voice would have no place there, and that was the thing I savoured more than anything else, the idea that my voice might be silenced at last.

The fat-man doesn't wait for an answer. He goes into the sitting room, munching on the chocolate bar.

I consider what the final scene might be. He hears the hum of the car before I do, it purrs softly like a cat and then it stops, I know he's parking the luxury car some way down the road. Nevertheless the fat-man can see him through the sitting-room window, walking the rest of the way. He fetches the poker from the fireplace and hides behind the kitchen door. I imagine I find the strength in myself to muster a smile for when Mr Gatt knocks and enters. I want him to suspect everything is not as he had imagined it would be. Anyhow he only has a moment to see me and be shocked and horrified by the withered state I am in before the fat-man steps out from behind the door and smashes the back of his head in.

Meanwhile the fat-man has come back into the kitchen. He is excitable. He seems to have taken on a new lease of life. I feel my heart slowing down, the beats becoming few and far between, as if in direct proportion to the quickening of his pulse. Calm down, I want to say to him. I form a picture of my heart in my mind and I try to imagine it beating faster, but how long can I hope to keep that up for? Anyway I am soon distracted.

He's coming, the fat-man says.